STEAMING INTO THE BLITZ

More Tales of the Footplate in Wartime Britain

Michael Clutterbuck

HEDDON PUBLISHING

First edition published in 2019 by Heddon Publishing.

Copyright © Michael Clutterbuck 2019, all rights reserved.
No part of this book may be reproduced, adapted, stored in a retrieval system or transmitted by any means, electronic, photocopying, or otherwise without prior permission of the author.

ISBN 978-1-913166-01-4

Cover design by Heddon Publishing.

Cover image courtesy of the Great Western Trust.

This is a work of fiction. Names, characters, businesses, places, events and incidents are either the products of the author's imagination or used in a fictitious manner. Any resemblance to actual persons, living or dead, or actual events is purely coincidental.

www.heddonpublishing.com
www.facebook.com/heddonpublishing
@PublishHeddon

This series is dedicated to my late father, William Harold Clutterbuck, himself a railwayman. In giving his son a Hornby train in 1937, he passed on a bug which still claims me firmly. My only regret is that he is no longer with us to see the results. Thank you Dad, for all you did for us.

Introduction

Since *Steaming into the Firing Line* was first published in 2012, there have been requests for another book on the same period. Most of the incidents related are based on events which really did occur during the Second World War; mainly, although not entirely, in and around London, and were often caused by the strains and stresses of working under the attention of the Luftwaffe, and later the V1 and V2 attacks.

It has always seemed to me a shame that while the Armed Forces in wartime are frequently reflected in fiction, the plight of railwaymen has been largely neglected. What the railwaymen had to put up with, like the activities of the police, the fire services and other civilian organisations during the Second World War in the UK, has hardly been given a mention. It has been therefore my intention in a minor way to try and correct this imbalance.

I was born just before the war and had a father who served through this difficult period in a clerical capacity. He was too old to be called up and his boss refused his application to join up. In any case, he was, like almost all railwaymen, in a Reserved Occupation. The family rarely saw him at this time as he was in the office during the day and out at night with the Air Raid Precautions organisation (ARP). We children only saw him on the weekends. His war medal was awarded for his service to the War Savings programme. Those readers who would like further details of the railways' war efforts could do a lot worse than get hold of a copy of Michael Williams' *Steaming to Victory* which gives a fine overview of the topic. The railway companies themselves also published accounts of their own activities at the time.

Most of the episodes related in this collection are only partly fictitious. The ammunition train explosion was not on the GWR: it was at Soham in Cambridgeshire, and only two railwaymen were killed, with one wagon destroyed. The driver's mistake regarding the track he was on (and the reasons for this error) did occur and led to some loss of life, but it was on the GWR, not the LMS. And those sceptics who scoff at the thought of an ancient locomotive fighting and defeating an enemy aircraft should look up the record of the Southern Railway's D3 0-4-4T tank engine No. 2365 in November 1942!

Steaming into the Blitz
More Tales of the Footplate in Wartime Britain

1 - The Evacuation Special (1st Sept 1939)..........................1
2 - The trains must go through (August 1940) 8
3 - The luck of the Irish (October 1940).......................... 15
4 - No safety for clerks (December 1940)........................ 21
5 - Away from the Inferno (March 1941) 27
6 - The Tunnel of Love (May 1941)................................ 33
7 - Two useful bins (July 1941) 40
8 - A train of events (September 1941) 46
9 - UXB (March 1942)... 52
10 - A tiny railway declares war (April 1942) 59
11 - The Troops are not amused (August 1942) 66
12 - An engine bites back! (September 1942)................... 72
13 - A railwayman's dilemma (February 1943) 78
14 - A breath of fresh air (October 1943)......................... 85
15 - No Immunity for visitors (November 1943) 91
16 - The female of the species (February 1944) 98
17 - The ammunition train (March 1944) 105
18 - V is for vengeance (June 1944) 111
19 - A train to suffer in (July 1944)............................... 117
20 - Suffocation (Jan 1945)... 123
Technical vocabulary.. i

1 - The Evacuation Special (1st Sept 1939)

In late August 1939, the announcement came through that astounded the nation: the Russians and Germans had concluded a mutual non-aggression pact. That these two hitherto hostile powers could agree on anything was a complete shock. It horrified the French and British governments, who immediately realised it could drastically alter the military balance in favour of Hitler's Wehrmacht. He need no longer fear, at least in the immediate future, an attack on two fronts. It also gave him what he had been waiting for: the opportunity to invade Poland without fear of Russian interference.

The effect on the British people was immediate. The long-projected procedures to move children away from towns thought to be targets; particularly London, but also other large cities like Birmingham, Manchester, Glasgow and Newcastle, were quickly set in motion.

The impact on the Big Four railways was also immediate. At the beginning of September, Waterloo Station was heaving with children and their mothers, alongside Southern Railway officials who were trying to arrange for the youngsters to board the trains out of the capital. Many of the children were excited by the change of routine but others were frightened at having to leave their parents, most for the first time in their young lives. The instructions had gone out that on 1st September the evacuation of children from the capital should begin, in case of war and a sudden attack by air.

Other London termini were also involved: Euston, Paddington, King's Cross, Victoria and St Pancras all had their crowds of children and anxious parents wondering when they would see ever each other again. In spite of the forward planning by the railways and the government, the evacuation procedures placed an almost impossible burden on the railways, which were expected to conduct their normal business in addition to this extra imposition. Only the older officials in all departments realised that this unreasonable burden was going to be the lot of the railways for the foreseeable future; they had seen it all before, during the Great War. They knew that overcrowded passenger trains, heavy goods trains and long periods between vehicle maintenance would follow.

"I don't know why there's all this fuss," grumbled old Ernie Becker, leaning out of the cab window of his Southern Railway 2-6-0 Mogul class general purpose mixed traffic locomotive at Waterloo. He was watching for the starting signal, which would let him depart with his eight-coach 'Special', crowded with evacuees heading for Salisbury, Exeter and Barnstaple, to deposit the children into a variety of ostensibly safe havens.

"They talk o' bombs on London," replied his fireman, 'Geordie' Wilkins. Geordie's real name was Bartholomew and he came from Newcastle, but his accent was so thick that his colleagues found him sometime very hard to understand, hence the nickname.

"Well, we've seen them before," replied Ernie.

"Aye, we 'ave an' all, but this time the bombs'll be bigger."

As they were talking, a little lad came up the platform and called out to Geordie as he was leaning out to watch the crowd.

"Hey, Mister, where's yer train goin'?"

"We're goin' ter Barnstaple, bonnie lad; are yer comin' with us?"

At this moment, however, a large lady with an armband came huffing and puffing up to them. "Come here, Jeffrey Mitchell, you little devil! You come straight back to your group and don't you let me catch you running off again."

She grinned at Geordie. "You've got to watch 'em all the damn time," she said as she grasped little Jeffrey by the collar of his coat. "This one's to be sent to the quiet countryside around Basingstoke, but if I don't watch him he'll be away again and they'll find him in Salisbury or Exeter, where there'll be nobody to meet him." She dragged him back to her small group of children, all with their cardboard gas mask boxes and cases, and some with name labels hanging round their necks. She chivvied them into their allocated coach, counting them as they went in.

Geordie turned to his mate, who had moved over to watch. "I don't envy 'er 'avin' to keep an eye on a dozen lively nippers, Ernie," he said, shaking his head. "My son's a teacher in Jarrow and 'e sez that lookin' after a crowd of kids out o' school is the 'ardest thing in teachin'; it's like trainin' cats. Giv' 'em 'alf a chance and the little buggers are racin' off in all directions."

Ernie chuckled. "Lucky all you have to do, Geordie, is to shovel a few tons of coal into the firebox, and not chase sprogs all over the place."

As they were discussing how to handle children, the guard's whistle blew and Geordie checked the starter signal on the platform.

"All clear to go, Ernie."

Ernie Becker gave a quick glance at the dials on the backhead as he heaved on the regulator and the engine began to move off with its train. The two crewmen busied themselves in the cab as they cajoled their train slowly out of Waterloo; an electric eight-car set accelerated past them with contemptuous ease, on its way to Portsmouth. Their little Mogul had eight coaches heavily loaded with evacuee children and their minders, and was working hard, but by the time they were passing Vauxhall, it had its train under steady control and it was able to pass through Clapham Junction at speed, without any signal check, on their way to the first stop at Basingstoke.

Some eighty-three minutes later, they slowed and drew to a gentle stop to disembark the first group of evacuees. Geordie, looking back out of the cab, saw the same lady leading her group on the platform towards the exit and he noticed she had little Jeffrey Mitchell firmly by the collar;

she wasn't taking any chance of him escaping her clutches once again. She met another lady and, still holding the lad, handed her papers over. They jointly counted the children, calling out names as they did so. Geordie saw how she was careful to pass the lad over to her counterpart and indicate that he needed watching.

Another lady had also left the train and had passed her group to a second official. The train guard, having spoken to both women, turned, blew his whistle and waved his green flag to signal the 'all clear'; they could proceed. As the starter signal had already dropped, Geordie nodded to his driver and the latter took hold of the regulator to open it gently.

At that moment, there was a loud shout and a piercing whistle. Ernie quickly looked out of the cab, closed the regulator and slammed on the emergency brake, bringing the train to a lurching halt instantly.

"What's up, Ernie?" The surprised Geordie looked at his driver.

"Dunno, Geordie; the guard's waving his red flag urgently! Go and 'ave a look."

Geordie scrambled rapidly down onto the platform and hurried along the train to where the guard was standing by an anxious lady with a small group of children. "What's the problem, Jack?"

"One of the kids has vanished, it appears," muttered the guard.

"'Ave they looked everywhere, like in the bog?"

"Yep, seems so."

"Did the kid get off the train?"

The guard looked questioningly at the lady, who shook her head. "No, she didn't."

"Well," said Geordie, "she must still be in the train somewhere. What does she look like?"

"She's only six, small with blonde hair and a blue jacket and a dark red skirt."

"Like that little girl with those children in the next coach?" asked Geordie, pointing to a group of heads sticking out of the window.

"Oh good heavens, yes that's her! Thank you so much. She must have wandered into another coach."

Two minutes later, the train was back on the move, with Ernie Becker trying to make up the lost ten minutes before the next stop at Andover Junction. However, they were hardly fifteen minutes away when without warning the brakes went on again and the train ground rapidly to a stop.

"Someone must have pulled the emergency cord!" exploded Ernie angrily. "Nip out, Geordie, and find out from the guard in which coach the cord was pulled and why."

Geordie nodded and was back in the cab a few minutes later. "A kid climbed up to get 'is bag from the rack, slipped and grabbed at the cord to stop 'isself from fallin'," he explained.

Ernie took out his watch. "We're thirty minutes late now already. That little sod has cost us twenty minutes' delay."

By Salisbury, they had managed to recover ten minutes, but lost them again at the platform because one official took her group of children out of the train under the impression that they were in already in Crewkerne.

"Can't she bloody read the station name-board?" exploded Ernie. "What kind of idiots do they get to look after these kids?"

But by the time they had reached Exeter and had offloaded over a hundred-odd more children, Ernie had succeeded, by dint of pushing the little 2-6-0 rather faster than it was used to, in recovering most of the lost time, and they were now only three minutes down.

They were allowed more time than normal for the final section on the run through north Devon so that children could be deposited at Crediton and Yeoford Junction, as well as at their final destination of Barnstaple. Five coaches had been taken off at Exeter so the Mogul had only three on over the remaining hilly section across, but Geordie was worried by the small amount of coal left in the tender and hoped they would have enough to manage the rest of the journey.

"Should be able to get to Barnstaple right time now," remarked Ernie to his fireman.

But in this he was to be seriously in error. With the end of the journey approaching, the previous care was beginning to relax. The children, after the two incidents at Basingstoke, had been strictly controlled, but were getting both tired and hungry; many had long since eaten their sandwiches. The chocolate machine on the platform at Crediton enticed many to escape their guardians and a long queue formed. It took another twenty minutes to chivvy them back into their seats and even then, three proved to be missing and another ten minutes were wasted before they were found in the station toilet.

At Yeoford Junction, the Stationmaster was called: a child had had a sliding compartment door slammed shut against his hand, and an ambulance had to be called to take him to the hospital. This lost them another hour, with all the noting down of the details for the report. A further problem occurred as the last two coaches were non-corridor coaches; these had been planned for the children to detrain at Basingstoke, as they would not have needed access to the toilets. They had been filled by mistake with children destined for Barnstaple instead, and these children were by now desperate to visit the toilet at the station. At least, those who had managed to hold out were; and those who had wet themselves (or worse) had provided their compartments with a rank smell, which brought tears to the eyes of station staff.

A very relieved Driver Becker and Fireman Wilkins finally brought their train to a halt in Barnstaple, more than two hours late. The last of the children were collected by their respective guardians and the railway officials took over the coaches of the train for cleaning. These were shunted into a siding and as the two crewmen walked to the shed to come off shift, Geordie Wilkins made a grave error, inspecting one of the coaches.

He reported what he saw to his driver. "You wouldn't

believe the mess in them coaches, Ernie, I've bin in pig sties that smell better!" He shook his head, "An' the war 'asn't even started yet!"

He was to recall this predicament some ten months later at Waterloo, after he had crewed an ambulance train from Dover, with exhausted soldiers returning from Dunkirk.

2 - The trains must go through (August 1940)

It was a tense time in Britain. There was immense and surprised relief that most of the British Expeditionary Force, and even a sizeable portion of the French Army, had been rescued from Dunkirk. It gave the army a basis from which to rebuild its strength. Yet, at the same time, the country was watching as the German Wehrmacht marched its triumphant way across France, achieving its occupation by Hitler's troops. Hitler had now taken Poland and Denmark, thrown the British willy-nilly out of Norway, and followed this up by seizing control of Luxemburg, Holland and Belgium, ending with the invasion of France. He appeared to be unstoppable and, equally clearly, Britain was next. All Hitler had to do was to keep the Royal Navy away and render the RAF harmless, so that neither could interfere with his invasion plans. RAF bases, therefore, had to be destroyed ready for the invasion and railways and other communication facilities had to be cut.

Driver Graeme Peters, born in 1905 into a working-class family, had won a scholarship to a prestige school in the north-west of England. Here he had prospered but had been unhappy at the snobbish attitude of his fellow scholars towards the labouring classes. Nevertheless, he had done well and won another scholarship, this time to an Oxford University college. But finding here the same kind of attitude that had upset him at school, he had abandoned his degree, retaining only his acquired cut-glass accent, and found greater satisfaction in working among his own class of railwaymen. His above-average education had resulted in him being conferred the good-natured nickname of 'the Professor' among his workmates at the Neasden engine shed in north London.

Fireman Bertram Harris was the complete opposite of

Driver Peters; Harris had been expelled from school at the age of thirteen, then joined the LNER as a cleaner. He had gradually worked his way up the link until he was a passed fireman, meaning he could also be used as a driver under restricted circumstances. He discovered early a liking for working in the cab of a steam locomotive, and was popular among the drivers due to his apparent instinct for knowing what to do in all circumstances. His sunny disposition made him doubly welcome in the cab.

When they were teamed up together for the first time, both Driver Peters and Fireman Harris had taken a strong disliking to each other but over their first week together they had both learned to appreciate the good humour and sterling qualities the other possessed. Whenever they came into mess rooms at shed, other enginemen pricked up their ears to listen to the entertainment. The conversation between the two men was always diverting: the mellifluous Oxford accent of the driver contrasted strongly with the north London cockney variety of his fireman. But in spite of occasional insults between the two men, the grins on their faces belied any animosity.

One morning, Driver Peters entered the enginemen's cabin with his fireman in tow. "Purloin that seat for me please, Bertram, while I peruse the board to study our duty this splendid morning." There were anticipatory smiles on a few of the nearby faces.

"Yessir!" replied the fireman as he walked over to the nearest bench. "Move yer arse," he growled at an engineman, "'Is Lordship wants ter park 'is bum there!"

But just before Driver Peters could sit down, Fireman Harris held up his hand to stop him.

"'Arf a mo'," he wiped his hand carefully over the surface of the bench. "Sir mustn't go on duty wiv mucky pants!"

"Thank you, my man; now a glass of tea with lemon would suit nicely," nodded Bert's driver, pointing to the counter where a tea lady was at work.

"Mug o' char, luv," said Bert to the lady. "The bugger's got a thirst!"

Ten minutes later, Graeme Peters pulled out his watch and remarked, "It appears that we have about eighty minutes to prepare our B17 class 4-6-0 for an early visit to the delightful city of Leicester. We shall depart to examine our mode of haulage."

"Fine," replied Fireman Harris, "You 'ave a butcher's at yer load ov oilage me Lord, and I'll go an' prepare our injin."

They left the cabin among chuckles from other enginemen.

"Righto, Bertie, let's get her ready." Without an audience, the conversation got back to serious business. Graeme Peters was a fine driver and he and Bertie Harris worked very well as a duo; they had been together for the last seven months and were comfortable with each other.

They backed the engine up the line to Marylebone and onto their ten coaches, to work the semi-fast to Leicester.

"Hope they give us one o' them D10s for the return trip, Prof," said Bertie, "but I once come back firin' a B7. They tole me it were on'y used on fish trains, but it 'andled our express orright. Still, I like them D10 4-4-0s, too; they're nippy and stronger than you'd fink."

"Indeed, I have driven a few and I concur with your opini–"

"Hey Prof, look at that plane; is it one of ours or is it a nasty Jerry lookin' fer a train ter bomb?" Bertie Harris had spotted a high-flying aircraft above them.

"Now, why is it doing that, I wonder?" replied his driver. "It's circling round to the left. Furthermore, I believe it is hostile."

The aircraft was still high but Graeme didn't like the look of it; a British aircraft wouldn't hang around in such a manner. "I am not happy, Bertie," he said, "I believe that aircraft is a German bomber looking for a target. Get ready for an emergency stop!"

But as he spoke, the aircraft commenced a dive at something well ahead of them and slightly to their right. They saw the bomb released, followed by a huge explosion somewhere ahead.

"Gawd, that's our bloody bridge!" shouted Bertie as Driver Peters dropped the regulator and applied the emergency brake.

There were squeals and sparks from the coach wheels as the brake shoes took hold, and the train gradually shuddered to a stop only tens of yards from the shattered bridge.

Both men stared at the wreckage. The bridge was totally cut and mangled, broken rails dangling down into the valley and over the road below.

"We could be somewhat tardy with our arrival in Leicester," commented Graeme Peters drily. "Bertie, you had best make your way at maximum speed to the box we just passed and inform its guardian of this piece of Teutonic savagery."

"I can certainly tell the bobby there the bridge is bust, but the phone line's down an' all, an' 'e can't warn any up trains comin' this way."

"No need to worry, Bertram, the other bobby will have seen or heard the explosion and will have noticed that his line's down. He will have stopped all up traffic."

Bertie nodded and raced off back up the line.

In the event, they were fortunate. The bobby in the next down box had stopped the next up train, a slow goods for Neasdon, from proceeding to its demise. But the destruction of the bridge had severed the whole line and all trains from Marylebone to the north, servicing Manchester, Nottingham and Sheffield, had to be diverted via High Wycombe and Princes Risborough on the Great Western/LNER joint line.
This caused further problems for the GWR, as this section was part of their own main line to Birmingham and Birkenhead, and was always very busy.

Back in the mess room, Driver Peters was relating their experience to a group of enginemen. "The aircraft was circling widdershins when it began to—"

He was interrupted by his fireman, "Oh gawd, the man's

swallowed a dictionary agin. Wot the 'ell are yer talkin' abaht? Wot's widows-wotever it was?"

"It means, you ignoramus, going round anti-clockwise, or, to be more precise, going round to the left. Very useful in certain spheres of activity."

"What spheres of activity, f'rinstance?" a driver wanted to know.

"Let us consider the following; imagine that a good friend of yours, perhaps George here," pointing to the next fireman, "has seriously hampered Bertram's general euphoria."

"E's wot?" Bertie frowned.

"To put it crudely: he's done the dirty on you. What are you going to do about it?"

"I'd punch 'is lights aht!"

"Yes, I'm sure you would, Bertram, but while punching his lights out is fine for immediate and brutal gratification, wouldn't you rather undertake a more lasting penalty for such an infraction of your happiness?"

"Wot lastin' penalty?"

"An irritating toothache, perhaps; a loss of hair, or a bad case of diarrhoea?"

"Cor, I like that!" said Bertie Harris with enthusiasm, "giv''im the shits fer a month! That would er, er—"

"Firmly curb his wellbeing?"

"Yerr – I think so," said Bertie, wondering whether he had understood. "But 'ow would I do that?"

"Simple. Witchcraft! You make a little image of George, place it on the ground, walk round it three times widdershins, and mutter suitable curses. All the best wizards and witches walk widdershins when casting their spells. As I remarked earlier, a very useful word. And now let us depart; our steed surely awaits."

They left amidst the appreciative grins of the remaining enginemen.

On their shift the next day, as they took the semi-fast to Leicester along the Great Western tracks, Bertie said, "It'll take flamin' weeks to rebuild that bridge!"

"Yes, they will have to, er, what is that coarse expression

– 'extract the digit' – to restore the service. But one never knows, we might be surprised," replied Graeme.

Although both men possessed the knowledge of the alternative joint LNER/GWR route, it was strange for Graeme and Bertie to find themselves driving past the Castles, Kings and Hall class engines of the GWR for the next few days. But both men possessed the route knowledge of the alternative route. However, they were astounded to read the train notices eight days later. They were booked to Leicester once more via Aylesbury, with a note that a 5mph speed restriction was in force over the bridge.

"But they can't 'ave rebuilt that bridge in eight days!" Bertie Harris turned to his driver.

"Unlikely, I know," murmured Graeme, "yet the train notice is perfectly clear concerning the matter. We shall have to see."

And see they did. As they approached the bridge, an up local passenger train hauled by an L1 4-6-4T tank engine passed them, accelerating towards Marylebone. As they slowed down to the required 5mph, they saw an army of builders and engineers working on the bridge, with scaffolding everywhere. Both up and down tracks had been repaired and the main supporting girders were in place. All details of the road and the valley sides, however, were clearly visible between the rails because there was as yet no infill of timber decking; this would take another couple of weeks, an official replied to their shouted enquiry as they eased their train over the skeleton framework the bridge.

"I don't bloody believe it!" Bertie shook his head as they picked up speed again beyond the bridge. "Indeed," agreed Graeme, "it does seem remarkable; nevertheless, it has happened."

Back in Neasdon shed a fortnight afterwards, they met a civil engineer who gave the enginemen a short explanation about the reconstruction. "A year ago we'd have had bitter union complaints about exploiting the workers but now the chips are down, it's very different."

Over the next five years, British railwaymen got used to seeing major damage repaired in ways and timescales which before the war would have been regarded as frankly impossible. Important bridges received instant attention in order to allow the trains through; other installations were also repaired in very short order. They also noticed that many of the vital nodal points of the system were guarded against possible sabotage, the railways themselves providing a few of the guard as part of the Local Defence Volunteers, widely known as Dad's Army.

3 - The luck of the Irish (October 1940)

Sergeant Liam O'Reilly had always considered himself to be a lucky man but he was wondering at this moment, just outside the French village, whether his luck had finally run out. Although Sergeant O'Reilly was born in Limerick in County Clare, he had, like many Irishmen from the Republic, joined the British Army and been sent to France with the British Expeditionary Force.

It was very dark and he could hear German soldiers rather closer than he would have liked. He assumed they were looking for him. In early May, his unit had been stationed a few miles south of Cherbourg, defending a bridge over a small river. As the German panzers approached, his unit had waited until one of the tanks was on the bridge before they blew it up and the other panzers were unable to cross. However, the Germans had had a pioneer unit with them and, while enemy soldiers had kept his troops occupied, the pioneers had quickly built a makeshift bridge a half-mile away, crossed it and attacked the British from behind, capturing most of them. Sergeant O'Reilly had escaped and had indeed, with passable French, been able to avoid capture for over four months. He had stolen a few items of clothing to cover his uniform and had also even found occasional work posing as a Flemish worker, trying to reach home without the attention of the authorities. But in this French village close to Dunkirk, he had run into a *gendarme* who actually spoke Flemish and who had tried to arrest him, thrusting a pistol into his back to march him to the *gendarmerie*.

This had been a mistake, as the sergeant had some skill in unarmed combat and had relieved the man of his pistol, then tied him up and locked him in his own cell before escaping once more. However, now that it was night-time, the Germans had obviously been alerted and the search was on.

Assuming the Germans might have dogs with them, he made his way several hundred yards along a small creek leading towards the coast. At about midnight, he came across a small fishing settlement. The smell told him he was close to the sea and he glimpsed a tiny harbour, where there were several fishing boats. One of the boats contained a tarpaulin, under which were three cases of brandy. Perhaps, he thought, his luck had not deserted him after all: this was a smuggler's vessel.

Twenty-four hours later, he was in Hastings. The local police station put him into contact with the army and, after spending some time with army intelligence in London, he was given three weeks' leave with his accumulated back-pay before he was ordered to rejoin his unit.

With no immediate family to visit, he elected to stay in a bed & breakfast in central London and learned of the necessity of spending the night in the underground system during the constant air raids. In the station, he found the noise of some of the families on the platform very disturbing and decided that a ten-yard trip with his blankets into the tunnel allowed him the sleep he badly needed. Having spent so many weeks sleeping rough, lying down below the rails snug in his blankets was no problem at all and he slept soundly until the mornings.

Many Tube stations in central London would have their platforms, and sometimes even their tracks, filled with sleeping locals; the emergency flood doors near the Thames would be shut, and maintenance work in the tunnels could begin. Most of the crowds in the stations were cheerful and used to the noise; some found it irksome but it was better than the alternative of staying up at street level to face the bombing. It would still be a while before the gossiping groups and the occasional mouth-organ players would cease their activities, and the children could be persuaded to go to sleep.

"Mind the doors!"

Motorman Harry Becket heard the cry of the guard above

the hubbub of the dozens of chattering people on the platform, most of whom were not *bona fide* passengers; many were already laying out their blankets in readiness for the night shut-down of the system, to give them a night's sleep away from the Luftwaffe's bombs.

"Mind the doors!" came the call again and Harry waited for the signal at the entrance to the tunnel; it turned green and he grabbed the handle and turned it, to begin the run to the next station on the Central Line. His was the last train of the day and once it had reached the end of its run it would be stabled and the power along the line would be switched off until the early morning.

As his train ran into central London stations, Harry saw the rows of sleeping bags, mattresses and cushions lining the platform, their owners settling down for the night. The few men in various uniforms were in the minority; most of the station's occupants were women, many with children of all ages. Some were settling down, while others were playing with the toys they had brought with them to while away the time before the lights dimmed. There were no longer many actual passengers, most having already reached their destinations; people did not walk the streets much at night. It was no longer safe, due to the Blackout and, it had to be admitted, to the thieves who plagued the darkened streets, risking injury or death from bombs against the almost certain chance of extorting a few shillings out of some passer-by foolish enough to risk a broken nose or even a knife in the ribs. The newspapers boasted of the new mood of public co-operation under the bombing but the police knew different: the crime rate among the night streets, like the traffic accident rate, was soaring, as the criminals found the lack of street lighting very much to their liking.

All these thoughts were running through Harry's mind as his train began the slight downhill grade leaving the station. Many underground stations had been built at a level just a few feet higher than that of the tunnels. This was to slow the arriving trains, thus assisting them in their braking before stopping and, equally, to help them accelerate after leaving the stations. In the almost forty years since most of the Tube had been in existence, it had been estimated that this simple procedure had saved the original companies, and then later London Transport, many thousands of pounds in brake-maintenance costs.

But a new development followed the airborne attacks on London as the public discovered that the underground could provide a safe environment at night. After some initial objection, the authorities had learned to tolerate this and now it was common, although not always as safe as it seemed.

One night, as Harry ran his train into Lancaster Gate for the day's last service, a soldier standing at the platform edge jumped in front of his cab. Harry had no time to use the emergency brake and his train hit the man's body at some speed. The soldier was killed instantly. At the subsequent inquiry, it was disclosed that the man had been in Dunkirk, where he had lost his right arm, and had returned home to discover his wife of eight months had moved into the flat of a previous boyfriend. All motormen knew that such incidents happened, although it was rarely reported, and was a constant fear in the job. Some men had to give up driving after experiencing a suicide, but Harry tried hard to accept the blow and was back at work the following day, endeavouring to control the tenseness that he felt.

Sleep on the platforms overnight was often disturbed by drunks, excited children, or loud snorers, and it was far quieter a few yards into the tunnel. Anyone foolish enough to venture into the tunnels, however, would need to be out again before the rails were re-energised early in the morning: the 600 volts in the live rails were lethal. On his first morning trip, Harry was always watchful in central London, and it saddened him to see so many families with their children for their overnight vigil.

Outside the city centre, things were relatively quiet; Harry himself lived well out of London, in Chigwell, Essex, where some kind of normality still reigned. This, however, was about to change.

Harry's work on the Central Line during the day kept him mostly ninety feet down under London, but one trip he had recently made as a passenger on the Metropolitan Line had demonstrated that travelling underground in central London was not always as safe from the bombing as one might expect. Their train had passed a huge hole, twenty feet across, into the street above; a bomb had punched through to the tunnel and the pile of rubble had been shovelled to one side of the tracks before it could be removed and the trains could run safely past. District and Metropolitan Lines had originally been built in the mid-nineteenth century using the 'Cut and Cover' principle, by which the streets had been dug up, the tracks laid and then covered over once more. This meant that they were much closer to the surface than the Tube lines (indeed, the Metropolitan Railway had been running its steam trains through from Paddington to the city by 1865; the line had been immediately popular, but the convenience of a fast passage under London had contrasted with the highly unpleasant smoke-filled stations and tunnels, and there had been great relief when it was finally electrified).

Such musings temporarily distracted Harry Becket's mind as his guard closed the doors and the train began to move, and he only caught a brief glimpse of the sleeping man under the tracks well into the tunnel as he accelerated rapidly downhill. He was at first too shocked to let go of the 'Dead Man's handle', as the safety device was known, and by the time he had applied the train's brakes, he was over and past the prone man under the tracks.

Sergeant O'Reilly had slept extremely soundly away from the noise on the station platform overnight, and the arrival of the morning's first train in the station had not at first disturbed him. It was only the approaching rumble of the wheels and the shaking of his surroundings which woke him up but his days on the run from the German occupying forces in France had taught him to wake and react instantly to danger.

"Jesus, Joseph and Mary!" muttered the startled soldier. But he realised at once that he was below rail-level and clear of the train's low-slung traction motors, and that therefore the train could not harm him if he stayed where he was. Then, once the train was past, he would rise very carefully, avoiding the live rails, and make his way back into the station. The train had stopped clear of him as he rose gingerly and made his way back to the platform, where the few passengers on the station were astounded to see him emerge unharmed. He threw his kitbag onto the platform and climbed after it.

Harry Becket was less fortunate. First, he had killed a man through no fault of his own, and now, less than a month later, he had run over another. It did not matter whether he had killed the second man, or whether the man had died from the 600 volts from the live rail as he rose from his slumber. All this was immaterial and even the fact, later discovered, that the soldier had survived made no difference to Motorman Harry Becket. He was no longer psychologically capable of driving an underground train. The London Passenger Transport Board transferred him to a position in one of its offices.

Sergeant Liam O'Reilly lived to fight on. He was popular with his men, partly because he was experienced and competent, but largely because he possessed one other rare quality, highly rated under battle conditions. He was a lucky man.

4 - No safety for clerks (December 1940)

The middle-aged businessman waiting with other passengers on a platform in New Street station in Birmingham turned to the lady standing next to him. "The trains are not as punctual as they were before this war started, are they?" he remarked.

The lady shook her head angrily. "I know we have problems with bombs but I really think they could do better," she said plaintively. "It's disgraceful the way the LMS run their trains these days! Do you realise that this London train is already twenty minutes late, and it even starts here! All they have to do is to fetch it from … wherever they keep their empty coaches, and they can't even do that on time!"

A few nearby passengers grumbled in obvious agreement.

After another fifteen minutes, the empty train steamed slowly into the station, pulled up at the platform, and was announced as the four-thirty to London Euston. Immediately, passengers scrambled to board the train with their suitcases, bags and sundry other luggage items and began to look for seats.

The train was soon full and late-comers were forced to stand in the corridors with their luggage on the floor next to them. The lady found herself in the same compartment as the elderly man she had been chatting to earlier. She leaned over to him and pointed to the people standing in the corridor. "Look at that," she said. "It's outrageous that they can't even put enough coaches on the train. I need to see my married daughter in Watford. I travel to see them every Christmas and stay for a week or so. How else is one expected to keep up with family matters? Surely they must know that people want to travel to see their families just before Christmas!"

"Your husband not travelling with you?" enquired the gentleman.

"No, he runs a grocery business, and a bomb damaged his warehouse last week so he has to find another source for some of the goods and hasn't the time to come with me."

The door to the corridor had been left open and a man in his thirties standing outside leaned in and spoke to the complaining lady. "I agree with you, madam, that the situation is outrageous, but if your husband's business is affected by the bombing, why do you imagine that the railways are not? I am a railway clerk and I can tell you exactly why this train does not have enough coaches. A bomb fell on our sidings last week and damaged the five extra coaches earmarked for this train. LMS management had nothing to do with it. You are lucky to have this train at all." He smiled. "Enjoy the visit to your family!" And he withdrew his head.

"You see what I mean?" The lady addressed the gentleman once more. "The railways don't seem capable of allowing for incidents like this and—"

She was interrupted by the man outside leaning through the door again. "We did have more coaches but they were sent south to Euston, to replace coaches damaged by an earlier raid." He nodded to the others in the compartment and slid the door firmly shut.

As the train moved out of New Street into the gloomy December day, the mood in the compartment matched that of the darkening sky. A small blue light came on, which only served increase the gloom in the compartment, as the window blinds were down in the Blackout.

"I wonder why that fella's not in the army?" Muttered an old man to the compartment in general.

"He's like me, I expect," remarked another man, "'Restricted profession'. I'm an off-duty police sergeant and they wouldn't let me join up, either."

There were silent nods in the compartment.

One of the greatest railway problems was the difficulty imposed by the Blackout in the marshalling yards. Since most of the heavy freight of the kingdom was transported by rail, it was necessary to have the yards working day and night. But at night, the yard lights drew the attention of the bombers, and therefore on the warning sirens the lights were doused, which of course caused immense disruption to the efficient functioning of the movement of goods through the country. The lights could not be turned on again until after the 'All clear' sirens sounded again. Shunters, drivers and firemen would have to cease their work, often for several hours, and, if the yard had been attacked, there could be severe damage to further hamper railway work. Some big yards could be put out of action for days, while craters could be filled, damaged rolling stock removed, and, if possible repaired, and tracks re-laid.

The air raid warning had sounded at Birmingham's Washwood marshalling yard and the railwaymen both there and at Saltley shed had taken rapidly to the shelters. Yard lights had been doused of course, but signal lights in the marshalling yard made it obvious to attacking Heinkels that this was the significant railway target they had been directed to attack. On this particular evening in mid-December, the yard was full of goods trains being shunted and re-marshalled. Amongst the innumerable vans and wagons, there were three coal trains from Nottinghamshire being remarshalled for forwarding to London for the capital's Christmas household fires; a freight train from Holyhead had arrived with potatoes from Ireland; two trains loaded with steel from the East Midlands were being divided for redistribution to local armaments factories; and an ammunitions train from the GWR in Wiltshire was waiting for an LMS locomotive to take it further on to Peterborough, and from thence via the LNER to the RAF in East Anglia. The Luftwaffe had picked an excellent night for their bombing raid.

In fact, the bombing was not as accurate as it might have been; the cloud cover had increased, thus rendering the raiders' bombsights less effective. Although the yard received many bombs, the damage was less effective than a 'bombers' moon' would have permitted. However, the surrounding areas had suffered considerable damage, and Luftwaffe planners would have been delighted to learn that they had inadvertently inflicted far greater impairment to the functioning of the LMS than an ordinary raid could have been expected to cause. Bombing a locomotive shed could put several locomotives out of action for a while, requiring temporary replacement locos from other sheds, and this would be a nuisance. But one of the bombs had scored a direct hit on the divisional office and killed and injured a score of clerical night-duty staff. Such specialists could not easily be replaced, and the loss dropped a far greater difficulty into the railway's lap. Control and timetable staff were, like the enginemen, trained experts, so replacement specialist staff were much harder to find. Consequently, the damage to the running of the division was far more serious. Passenger train connections failed, goods train routing was badly affected, and the cumulative effect was to disrupt the railway service for weeks.

The one fortunate aspect of the situation was that the Divisional Superintendent himself had actually been at a meeting in Euston during the raid on his offices in Birmingham. Henry Turner returned the following day, to find what was left of his department in chaos. All the night-duty staff had been affected, several killed; and those severely injured would be in hospital for some time, he was told. Only a few could be back at work within a fortnight.

Regrettably, his Chief Passenger Train clerk was one of the seriously injured, as was the Chief Control officer, and both of these men were vital to the smooth running of the division. At least their deputies had not been seriously hurt, and would be back at their desks within days.

The office buildings had been badly damaged, too, and the staff would need temporary accommodation until repairs could be arranged and all the phone lines reconnected.

Two days after the raid, Henry Turner picked up a phone at New Street Station and reported to Euston that he feared it would be at least two months before the division would be back to normal conditions.

On the passenger platforms below the offices, there was again vigorous discussion regarding the apparent failings of the LMS.

"You wouldn't credit it," a businessman was saying to a neighbouring passenger. "I have just come from Bristol and it took me five hours! *Five hours* from Bristol! And then I get here to find my connection to Nottingham left twenty minutes before my arrival. All this confusion just because a couple of bombs had fallen on the railway! These LMS timetables are hopeless. If they were in a library they should be shelved under 'Fiction'. How are we supposed to get around the country? I should have come by GWR instead, perhaps that would have been quicker."

"I doubt it," replied his neighbour. "I've just come up from Portsmouth via Reading and Birmingham Snow Hill. The GWR took three and a half hours for a two-hour journey. They're no better, and I have to get to Manchester to stay with my son and his family for the festive season."

The first man nodded. "Yes, Christmas with my daughter is what I am travelling for, and I have to say the railways aren't making it any easier."

He turned to the two young ladies standing near them. "And you, ladies, how do you find train travel these days?"

"It isn't easy, sir, I must say, but I'm not sure I blame the railways," replied the younger of the two.

"Oh?" said the first gentleman belligerently. "And why not, may I ask?"

"I think they are doing their best under very difficult circumstances," she replied.

"Doing their best? Do you call publishing a long-distance connection, and then making it impossible, doing their best?"

"But they can't help being bombed, surely?"

"No, of course not, but if an engine or a train is damaged, all they need to do is to fetch another one from somewhere. How hard is that?"

"And repair any track – that takes time," the second young lady added.

"Well, yes of course, but they have men to do that."

"Many of the men are now soldiers," she pointed out.

"Certainly they are, but they're now back in England after Dunkirk," he countered triumphantly.

"Many are in hospital," she replied.

"And you want soldiers to repair trackwork?" There was surprise in the second young lady's voice. "It's a job that requires skill and experience."

The two gentlemen looked at her in confusion. One of them commented, "You seem to know a lot about railway work, young woman."

She ignored the remark and continued. "Once you have the track and trains prepared, you need to make arrangements for the resumption of traffic. That can be complex because you have to allow for slower running; you can't have fast-running trains on recently repaired track. Just think, if an important train is now slower, you have to alter the timetable to allow for many connecting trains. For that, you need men experienced in complicated timetable work."

The two men looked at each other. "Who exactly are you?" one enquired of her.

"And what are you both doing here?" Queried the other.

"I have come from Wolverhampton to see my husband," said the first young lady.

"And I am from Daventry," said the other. "Bessie here and I are good friends, and our husbands work together."

"But your knowledge," interrupted the first gentleman. "How do you know all this technical information?"

"Our husbands are both in hospital. They are timetable clerks in the divisional offices and were badly injured in the raid. I hope you gentlemen enjoy your Christmases with your families."

5 - Away from the Inferno (March 1941)

"For God's sake, Beth, next time get yourself and James into the shelter at the first sound of the sirens!" Tom Simpson was worried that his wife might not take the bombing as seriously as he did. As an eight-year-old, he had been in London during the Great War, when bombs from the Zeppelins had fallen on the city; he had seen what they had done and he also knew that in the twenty years since, bombs would be far more devastating in their effects. But Beth was a country girl and he did not believe she could visualise exactly what could happen; she was an easy-going girl with a tendency not to panic. As a mother, this could be an admirable trait much of the time, but it had clear drawbacks if you lived anywhere close to a possible target and, if your house was less than half a mile from the London Midland and Scottish Railway's Camden locomotive shed, you were perilously close to a military target.

Beth nodded casually; "O' course I will, Tom, at the first wail."

Tom picked up his bag, dropped his waxed paper-wrapped sandwiches into it and headed for the door. "Make sure you do, love," he said as he left.

"Daddy seems a bit cross," commented nine-year-old James as he watched the tall figure of his father, in his blue boiler suit, stride down the narrow street past all the other doors and windows of the closely-packed terraced houses.

"Daddy worries and works too hard, Jimkin," said his mother as she packed the boy's lunch - also sandwiches wrapped in a bit of waxed paper - into his square cardboard box.

"But the box is for my gas mask, Mummy," complained the lad.

"Don't worry. Mr Hitler said they're not going to drop gas on us today," Beth assured the boy. "Now, run along, and I'll make sure you have your gas mask in the box tomorrow."

The boy nodded in satisfaction and went off to his school.

"Now, where on earth did I put that damn gas mask?" wondered Elizabeth to herself as she piled the breakfast things into the sink. She lit the gas on the stove for hot water to start the washing-up.

Fireman Redmond Wilkinson nodded to his driver as they met just outside Camden shed. "You look a bit out of sorts today, Tom, anything wrong?"

"No, Red, it's just that Beth doesn't understand the seriousness of the bombing. She's a bit slow in getting herself and the kids to safety when the sirens go."

"Mmm – that is a bit of a worry. Those bloody bombs aren't always on target; they often pepper the nearby areas. She really oughta see some damage for herself. I was in a complete bombed-out street in Wapping, visiting me cousin last week, an' you wouldn't believe how many houses a couple o' bombs can destroy."

"*I* know that and so do you, but I have to get it through to Beth, and I don't know how to."

They walked across the tracks, pausing as the massive streamlined shape of a grimy Coronation class 4-6-2 engine passed them, before carrying on to the enginemen's mess.

Red stopped suddenly and said, "Lissen Tom, I've an idea. What if I get me camera and photograph the street next time I go to see George? That should show her what bombs can do."

"Would you mind, Red? That 'ud be a great help; ta."

"I'll be seeing 'im again in a fortnight, Tom, just remind me to take me camera."

"I'll do that."

In the mess room, they noted they were booked, as expected, on a semi-fast to Rugby, with a Black Five 4-6-0 and ten corridors. The Black Five was a very successful general purpose engine and the ten coaches would not tax it unduly if it was in reasonable condition; but in this, the third year of the War, proper maintenance was no longer guaranteed. They could not be sure of its condition until they had backed down to Euston, coupled up to their train and run a few miles up the steep bank to Camden, by which time they would have got the feel of it. So, as they passed Carpenders Park, they were satisfied that the locomotive was in fair condition that should enable them to reach Rugby without any problems.

Fireman Wilkinson, however, was not entirely happy, his mate had almost overshot the platform at Watford Junction; something totally unlike his normal meticulous work. Tom Simpson was an excellent driver and to misjudge the length of platform with a train was very out of character for him. Redmond decided to keep a furtive eye on what his driver was doing for the rest of the trip. At Tring, Tom judged the platform length to perfection and also later at Bletchley; by the time of their arrival at Rugby, Redmond thought he might have been too hasty in assessing his driver's mental state.

Yet twice on the return to Euston, later in the day, he was careless: in a sudden rain shower on leaving Rugby, he started aggressively causing the engine to do a wheel-slip, which he instantly corrected. Then later passed a speed restriction, where permanent way men were relaying a siding at well above the designated speed limit. This latter error was serious and would certainly incur an embarrassing explanation, and perhaps even a hefty fine. It was so out of character that Redmond was convinced something was seriously troubling his mate.

A month later, they were moved to a new shift, which required them to go on to a turn as far as Carlisle with a sleeper train that would take on a new crew there and continue on to Glasgow. Their engine was an express passenger 4-6-0 Royal Scot class. As it was a tender engine, it had been supplied with a tarpaulin to be pulled over the gap between the cab and tender so that enemy aircraft passing overhead at night would not glimpse the light of the fire and attack.

As they were leaving Euston, they heard the sirens

beginning to sound. "Oh God, I hope Beth's getting herself and the kids into the shelter quick," muttered Tom, and Redmond noticed how uneasy he had become.

Racing through the night, they had got used to seeing pitch darkness everywhere, quite unlike what they knew from peacetime night runs. There were no street lights to be seen and even the cars showed only dim lamps. However, one advantage of the general blackout was that they could easily recognise the signals now that there were no other lights to distract them. Yet now traffic accidents were frequent and people had become very wary of night travel on the roads. On the blacked-out station platforms, white lines had been painted along the edges to make them easier to see in the dark.

Their run started badly as they were held up at Willesden for an hour due to an air raid, which meant that they had to crawl through the approach tracks while permanent way crews repaired some of the damage.

"Out of the Euston frying pan into the Willesden fire," commented Tom as they passed a set of sidings with a rake of shattered open wagons behind a derailed heavy 8F 2-8-0 goods engine.

"Hope the two crewmen got out in time as well as the guard," said Redmond as he watched for the signals allowing them entry into the station. "We're clear into the main down platform, Tom."

Watford was full of army personnel alighting and boarding the train even well after midnight, and the porters were also busy assisting passengers so that they could get the train away smartly to try and make up lost time. On this stretch of the line, there were four tracks with up and down main and slow lines. Express passenger trains would normally be sent on the down main, leaving the down slow for any goods or local passenger trains.

"Now we'll try and regain what we can," said Tom. "We're lucky that they're putting us on the down main and it's clear. Just check that we've got our tarp properly covering overhead so that any wandering Jerry aircraft doesn't spot our fire and drop a little present on us, Red."

Redmond checked. "Yep, it's on tight," he said as they left Tring, and then a surprised, "Crikey! They've routed us on the down slow." This was unusual, but not unknown if the traffic was heavy. Tom nodded absently, as he watched Redmond bending to shovel more coal into the firebox in readiness for the increasing demands of the locomotive's boiler. Although the Royal Scots were powerful express passenger engines, the big Pacifics were normally used on heavy sleeper trains, but their Scot was in good condition and soon they were accelerating to about 60mph, when Redmond noticed their speed and called, "Hey up, Tom, remember we're on the down slow!"

"Yes, yes," Tom replied absently then added, "we've already picked up seven minutes, Red, and—" He stopped in shock, seeing another train overtaking at high speed on the adjacent down main. "Christ!" he shouted when he realised where they were. "We're on the down slow!"

The overtaking express was well past and they were rapidly approaching a crossover on which the signals were re-directing him back onto the down main, behind the previous express; he urgently tried to slow down his train but he was far too late. They were still travelling at fifty-five when they reached the crossover to the down main, which was far too fast; the locomotive and tender derailed and tipped over, with the first five coaches also off the track.

Driver Tom Simpson was killed, as were seventeen sleeping passengers. The number of badly injured, a few of whom were not to survive the following week, reached forty-seven. At the subsequent inquiry, Fireman Wilkinson, still in his hospital bed, was asked how it was that Driver Simpson, with an exemplary record, had come to make such a basic and tragic error.

"He had been distracted for some time beforehand, sir," explained Redmond. "I think he had been very anxious about his family in the bombing. He was worried that his wife did not take the precautions as seriously as he felt she should, and I believe this fear for his wife and son played much on his mind. I warned him that we were on the down slow, but he can't have taken my warning in."

The inquiry concluded that the cause of the accident was negligence on the part of Driver Simpson, exacerbated by his recent history of long, heavy shifts. The pressure of domestic worries was taken into account, and since the man responsible had been killed, there was no purpose to be gained in any further action. He was clearly a victim of the War.

6 - The Tunnel of Love (May 1941)

The A4 Pacific, in its very grimy garter blue, the wartime all-over black paint scheme having not yet reached this engine, eased its train into the main up platform at Doncaster. It was on its way from Newcastle to King's Cross, and, like most passenger trains during the war, was very full. The platform was also full of passengers and included a number of RAF personnel from some of the Lincolnshire airfields, all trying to find space in the crowded corridors of the train; there hadn't been a spare seat since the departure from Newcastle. Emily Sanders and her friend Gertie French, both young WAAFs, were tired of standing in the corridor and looked despairingly out of the carriage window at the platform throng. Emily had a tall, slim figure, whereas her friend Gertie was more full-bodied. Both girls had a ready sense of humour, although at this moment it was rather lacking.

"Hardly anyone's getting off, Em," said Gertie sadly. "We got in at York and we're going to have to stay on our tootsies all the way to London."

"Never mind, Gert," replied Emily, "we'll find somewhere in London and enjoy a nice long kip, before we start our three days' leave. I know a fella there who'll be glad to give us a bed in exchange for a little cooking."

Gertie looked carefully at her friend, "I don't mind the bed provided I don't have to share it with some randy fella."

Emily laughed. "You won't need to worry about Ernest," she grinned. "He's not like that. Mind you, if your handsome brother George was with us, it'd be different!"

"Ah!" replied Gertie. "He's one of them, is he?"

Both girls had been in the Women's Auxiliary Air Force long enough to have met all types of men and did not share the resentment of homosexuals that many others harboured; indeed, they rather enjoyed their company, considering them generally safe and considerate companions.

By the time their train began to move again, however, they were eying with interest the two RAF officers edging along their corridor towards them. The two pilots, Flying Officer Marshall and Flight Lieutenant Harrison, were being sent south to transfer to their new fighter squadrons. The officers squeezed themselves alongside the girls in the corridor and put their cases down. "Here, ladies," said Sam Harrison, "sit yourselves down on our cases, we've still got some way to go to London. If you're going that far, of course."

"Thank you very much," replied Emily gratefully, "we've been standing since York."

Both girls settled themselves on the proffered cases; there was no danger of falling off them as the corridor was packed with standing passengers. The men introduced themselves but Emily and Gertie did not mention their WAAF status as there were strict regulations regarding relationships between officers and other ranks in the armed forces, and in any case the girls were not in uniform.

Curiously, enough passengers left the train at both Grantham and Peterborough so that the four of them were able to find seats together in one compartment. At Potters Bar, however, there was a long delay and their train rolled slowly into King's Cross just before midnight.

"Blimey," muttered Emily, "we'll not be able to get to Ernie's at Wimbledon tonight, Gertie. We'll have to kip in the station or somewhere."

"Leave it to me, ladies," Sam Harrison said. "I have an idea that will give you some privacy as well as a long and comfortable seat to sleep on till the morning."

"How will you do that, Sam?" asked Gertie curiously.

"Wait and see; Brian and I have been to King's Cross a few times already and we know how it can be done."

By May 1941, things at King's Cross were getting a little more organised for the bombing and when in the late evening the sirens began once more to sound their ululations, everyone would hurry to the nearest shelters, including military personnel of all kinds: British Navy, Air Force and Army uniforms would be seen on all platforms, interspersed with men from the Dutch, Free French, Norwegian, Polish and Czech armed forces. Civilians would also be about, although very few with children this late at night.

The late arrival from Newcastle disgorged its passengers, who joined the throng to the shelters, but the usual 0-6-2T N2 class tank engine, which would normally withdraw the coaches and take them to the coach sidings, had not arrived and the crew of the A4 locomotive had been ordered to push the coaches back into the Gasworks Tunnel, to ensure that at least one train could escape any bombs which might be dropped overnight. Parking trains in the Gasworks and Copenhagen Tunnels had become a common procedure at night, to guarantee some safety in the event of an air raid on the neighbouring stations of St Pancras and King's Cross.

But just as the platform starter signal dropped, the air raid sirens began their undulating wail. "Wouldn't you bloody know it?" grumbled Driver Worsley as he released the brakes, on hearing his mate Fireman Longman call out that the signal had cleared the road for them to back out.

The guard near the rear of the train noticed the RAF officer on the platform behind him. "The last coach is quite empty," the officer told him, "I've just been through it."

"Thank you, sir," said the Guard gratefully. "Saves me a few minutes checking." He turned to wave to the Driver to indicate that the train was empty of passengers. He hopped back into his guard's compartment and began switching all the coach lights off. He did not notice that the RAF officer had not passed him on the platform.

Back in the rear coach, as the lights doused, Sam Harrison switched on his little torch. "Righto, girls," he smiled, "we're safe from the bombing for a while, so let's get comfy! Now Brian," he addressed his friend, "dig out that little bottle I know you have in your kitbag!" Brian pulled out a large bottle of whisky, but a small packet came out with it and fell on the compartment floor.

"My, my," remarked Gertie, eyeing the packet. "You *are* well prepared: a couple of white party balloons, too!"

Driver Worsley had just eased the train into the tunnel when the first bombs began to fall, although he and his fireman thought they were falling rather on the LMS at neighbouring St Pancras, rather than on King's Cross itself. They had halted with their locomotive inside the tunnel, near the entrance, where they felt that they were relatively safe but could see what was going on.

One of the bombs scored a direct hit on St Pancras Station and they watched as great shards of glass and steel shot into the air.

"Cripes," exclaimed Jim Worsley, "think of all that beer under the station that might be lost! It doesn't bear thinking about!" St Pancras had a huge beer storage facility underneath the station platforms, which held the vast quantities of the drink, brought to the thirsty capital direct from the Burton breweries in Staffordshire.

The raid was a long one and they had to wait for over an hour before they were cleared to leave their train in the tunnel and bring their A4 into the shed for turning and servicing.

At the crack of dawn, a waiting N2 tank engine moved up to draw the teak coaches from the tunnel and stable them in the carriage sidings, ready for cleaning and preparing for their next duty. The N2 driver backed his engine toward the coaches, while his fireman waited on the bottom step of the cab for him to reach them. At the gentle nudge, as the engine contacted the buffers of the first coach, he dropped off and ducked underneath to check the automatic coupling had clicked into place, then he attached the vacuum pipe to the locomotive.

In adjacent compartments of the rear coach there was a sudden panic as the two couples woke up from the slight lurch as the engine buffed up to the coaches.

"Oh god, Brian, we've overslept!" called Sam. "Quick, girls, we've got to get out before the railway cleaners catch us. Just grab your things and let's vamoose!"

They dressed rapidly, grabbed their belongings, and hurried along the corridor to the end door. Flight Lieutenant Harrison glanced outside, saw the fireman and said, "No; the other side!"

They opened the opposite door, climbed gingerly down, and dropped the last few feet to the ground.

"Now, quickly but carefully, ladies, and don't let yourselves be seen until we reach the station platform!"

Neither crewman noticed the sudden departure of four silent figures scurrying along the tracks in the semi-darkness, and the two couples reached the platform unobserved. The officers took the girls to the station canteen, which was already open for the early morning commuters were beginning to arrive.

"Four teas and buns please, love!" called Brian to the canteen lady, handing her a florin, as his colleague escorted the girls to a seat.

"A quick bite and then I'm afraid we'll have to leave you both," said Sam. "We have to catch the Metropolitan to RAF Hornchurch."

"Well thank you, sirs, for a safe and comfortable night, with a little active entertainment thrown in for good measure!" chuckled Gertie as the two officers took their departure.

Soon after 6.00am, the cleaning ladies arrived at the carriage sidings with their buckets, brushes and mops, to work their way through the coaches. Two of them began with the front coach, and two walked along to the last coach to work their way back. Sixteen-year-old Annie Johnson in the last coach stopped in the corridor outside one of the compartments and called to her colleague, "Oi

Betty, come and 'ave a gander at this!"

Betty Purvis, her much older colleague, came out of the compartment she was cleaning and said, "What's up, Annie girl, what's got yer knickers in a knot?"

Annie pointed at the seats in the compartment she had been about to clean. "Talkin' o' knickers; someone's lost 'ers!" The two ladies cackled as they saw the evidence of the rapid exit: an RAF cap and a pair of lady's frilly panties on one seat; an empty whisky bottle and an RAF tie on the other, and another pair of smalls in another compartment. "An' 'ere's a white balloon," remarked Annie, pulling it out from under a seat. "Why would they want a balloon?" she wondered.

"Bin a bit of a party 'ere, I'd say, Annie!" said Betty, holding up the frilly panties. "Bin a long time since I fitted inter one o' them, but I remember when my Bert used ter try and get 'em off me when he'd 'ad a few an' – ah well, never mind, 'e's probably forgotten about them days by now!" she said with a grin. "And," she added, snatching the 'balloon' and dropping it into her rubbish bag, "that's no party balloon neither, Annie. You've still got a bit to learn! But wot we're lookin' at 'ere is a couple o' RAF types wiv their floozies, all nice and comfy in a dark tunnel, escapin' the bombin'!"

"But that's disgustin'!" said Annie indignantly. "RAF orficers be'avin' like that, and in the train too, an' 'ang on a mo – *your Bert?* Surely 'e didn't do anyfink like that? 'E's a gennellman."

"Yes, well we was all young once, Annie, an' 'ad our moments! You youngsters these days may be a bit faster with the war an' that, but don't ferget there was a war on when we was young, too. We also 'ad ter 'ave some fun, even if we didn't tell our parents everythin'!"

Annie stared at her older friend; she couldn't imagine Betty as a young, slim girl, flirting with an equally young, lecherous Bert in his cups, acting very much like some of the boys in her own age group she'd had to fend off. Then a startling thought struck her: if Betty and Bert had been like that, what about her own parents, who were of a similar age? Surely *they* hadn't been...?

"Oi!" Both ladies jumped at the angry shout as their foreman appeared in the corridor. "Wot the 'ell are you ladies playin' at? There's a train to clean 'ere! These coaches are due out again on the 8.15 Newcastle! You're supposed to be workin', not standin' around yackin'. Don't you pair know there's a war on?"

7 - Two useful bins (July 1941)

Fireman Fergus Johns and his mate Driver Jamie Melton had spent the day on the London–Southend run with their 4-4-2T tank engine and its six maroon painted, non-corridor coaches, taking city commuters to their places of work and back to their seaside homes. These old engines had been the mainstay in the early days of the London Tilbury and Southend Railway, and had been able to provide a fast commuter service to and from the capital; but with wartime conditions, the engines, some of them with over forty years of service, were no longer in prime condition. Added to the crowding and to the heavier weights of the trains, the engines could no longer be relied on for exact timing. Jamie and Fergus now much preferred the far newer William Stanier-designed 2-6-4T engines. Stanier had been a GWR man for most of his working life and had brought the best of the GWR's practices to the LMS, totally rejuvenating the LMS locomotive fleet with a range of successful engines, among which were these tank engines; they could easily handle the heavy commuter trains and had roomy and relatively comfortable cabs for their crews.

The two crewmen had taken their locomotive from Fenchurch Street station back to Plaistow shed to be stabled for the night and felt that it was surprising, as they prepared to walk home after their shift, how quickly one became used to the now daily scenes of devastation in the East End of London. Rows of terraced houses with great gaps in them like missing teeth, where enemy bombs had blasted homes and their human contents. Half-destroyed houses, pathetic with signs of open upper storeys; broken toilets, or precariously dangling wash basins; even twisted bed frames could sometimes be seen. Piles of brick rubble indicated where bombs had landed on houses instead of on the docks, at which they had presumably been aimed.

The corner shops could now mainly sell only their regular products which required ration coupons; buses and trams were often overcrowded, as workers hurried into the City to their factories and offices, most wondering whether their workplaces still existed after the overnight air raids. The only thing Driver Melton and Fireman Johns couldn't get used to was the fear that their own homes and families had been hit by the Luftwaffe.

The sirens began just as they were leaving the enginemen's mess room on their way home. They had walked less than twenty yards towards the exit when the first bomb fell near one of the passenger B12 class 4-6-0 engines, which was parked outside the works following a minor repair. Possibly, thought Fergus as he raced past, this engine would be back in the repair shop the next day. The two men were not hurt but there was no time to reach the nearest bomb shelter.

Fergus noticed the line of steel rubbish bins along a nearby wall. "Quick, Mr Melton, into one of those bins! It'll give us some protection from shrapnel!"

"We'll never get into one o' them bins, yer daft bugger!" shouted Jamie. "They're far too small!"

But Fergus ignored him, grabbed a bin, tipped the rubbish out of it and climbed in, drawing the lid over his head.

"Blimey!" a startled Jamie stared but when a second bomb dropped close, he too grabbed another bin, emptied the rubbish out, squeezed himself in and sank down, holding the lid over his head.

As they squatted inside their bins, three more bombs landed and the bins shook; there were frequent *pings* as small splinters bounced off the thin steel sides. The raid lasted only for about fifteen minutes but both men waited for the 'all clear', which sounded after another quarter of an hour, and then they struggled out.

"God, I never thought I'd get in there," muttered Jamie as he glared at the bin he had just climbed out of. "It looks far too small fer a bloke to get into. And look at them shards! Any of those hit us an' we'd 'a been shredded!"

"Let's see what other damage has been done to the shed," said Fergus, brushing his clothes down to clear some of the rubbish still adhering to his overalls. "God, I'll need a bath every day for a fortnight to get rid of this pong!"

Fergus was an unusual engineman, in that he had attended a local grammar school and his parents had assumed that he would pass his exams and find an office job 'with prospects', as they boasted to their friends. But Fergus had joined the railway when there were few jobs around, and found that he enjoyed the work, so he had stuck with it. He had already been promoted to Fireman and was hoping soon to move up to Passed Fireman, which meant that he could also drive, under a senior driver's supervision.

"My missus'll 'ave me guts fer garters when I get 'ome," complained Jamie, "an' when she smells me pong I don't even like ter think what she'll say!"

"Let's hope we've still got homes to go to," said Fergus grimly as they continued on their way back.

The two crewmen got on well, in spite of the huge difference in both age and education. Jamie appreciated his young fireman's enthusiasm and ability with the shovel and did all he could to help him in the ways and idiosyncrasies of the steam locomotive. Fergus, for his part, was pleased at having a senior driver who didn't treat him with the disdain that many young and inexperienced firemen met with when firing to a senior driver. The fact that both men lived in neighbouring streets and drank at the George & Dragon pub also helped to cement their friendship. Theirs was a closely-knit community of rows of terraced houses.

"Oh my Gawd!" muttered Jamie as they turned a corner into the street next to his; a stick of bombs had landed here and four of the houses had been effectively demolished, three more losing their roofs and much of their upper floors. Bedrooms with missing walls and hanging bed remnants could be seen. The street was strewn with household debris and two ambulances were already there, loading injured. Several policemen and the local fire brigade were assisting. A covered line of about a dozen bodies had been laid out for identification. Friends and relatives were making agonising discoveries and in tears informing the police of the details. Fergie recognised sorrowfully two of his drinking mates among the bodies, and stopped to check that the police knew their names. Jamie hurried on; he was worried about his wife and children, and Fergie ran to catch up with him in case he needed any moral support.

They were lucky. The next street was undamaged and when Jamie reached his house he found his wife and two teenage children shocked but unhurt.

"We was all in the shelter, Jamie," explained his wife, "An' your place is safe, Fergie," she added. "I went round to check, "'Arriet ain't hurt, she was took to the shelter in time." Harriet was Fergie's Siamese cat and he was very fond of her.

"Thanks, Mrs M, I'm very relieved to hear that. I'll get on home to see to her."

"Your neighbour, Mrs Leaton, is lookin' after 'er, so don't worry. Stop and 'ave a bite wiv us; you'll be knackered after your shift an' the bombin' an such. An' you've bin a mate of my Jamie's fer such a long time, fer Gawd's sake call me Mary!"

Fergie nodded. "Mary it is, Mrs M... Oh sorry, er, Mary!"

The laughter from everyone eased the tension of the situation for the moment but later, when five plates of 'bangers and mash' appeared round the table, the mood was again sombre and the little chat was meaningless, more to break the stillness than anything else. The children left to go to bed as it was by now close to midnight and Fergie made his own way home.

The scene at the shed the next day was one of what appeared to be controlled chaos; the newly or recently repaired B12 was back in the workshop, although on further investigation the damage had seemed worse in the heat of the moment than it actually was. No other engines had been damaged but several coal wagons had been destroyed and their loads scattered about. More serious was the damage to the tracks leading from the shed to the main line; until these could be brought back into operation, the whole shed was virtually out of use. This was a major difficulty for southern Essex, as Plaistow was a large shed and its locomotives provided a considerable fraction of the east London commuter services. Many of the enginemen were helping out with the repair gangs filling in the craters under the tracks in readiness for relaying. The greatest problem lay with the pointwork; much of this required specialised track parts to be brought in from the Permanent Way storage department and aligned with accuracy – not as simple a task as plain track. The senior foreman believed that they could have the link to the main lines back in action within two days; the gangers were resourceful men but they needed the specialist parts. In peacetime, the job would be much quicker, but they could not work through the night without floodlighting, and this was out of the question in the Blackout.

Two fitters walking past the row of bins just inside the shed entrance were flabbergasted at seeing two bins with the rubbish on the ground right next to them.

"Cor, look at that, 'Arry!" said one. "Look at what the bombin' did to them two bins! It shook out all the muck but left the lids on! How the holy hell did it do that?"

"Never seen the like," said his mate, equally bemused. "I've seen a coupla funny things in the bombin' but nuthin' like them two bins; an' why on'y two of 'em? All the others is still full o' rubbish!"

Puzzled, the two men went on to their work in the shed, discussing the peculiar phenomenon with their mates over lunch. They were working on the newly damaged B12 but were surprised to discover that most of the damage was actually in the form of dints in the boiler cladding, apart from a split in the right-hand cylinder cover; nothing that shed fitters couldn't handle with ease. It had also been derailed but again, that was a common enough occurrence at any shed, even in peacetime, and the engine was rerailed with jacks and another engine drawing it back onto the track.

Fergie and Jamie, in the meantime, had assisted with filling in the craters and with no engines able to leave the shed were now at a loose end. They walked back to the bins they had climbed into during the raid and stared at them.

"What the bloody hell are you two doin'?" A startled driver on his way out gazed as the two men were trying in vain to climb into the empty rubbish bins. Neither man was able to get even half-way and they climbed out sheepishly.

"Did we really get inside them?" said Jamie, shaking his head in disbelief.

"We damn well did," Fergie assured him.

"But 'ow?" asked Jamie. "I can't even get 'alf-way in now."

"You two got inside them bins in the raid?" demanded the driver in disbelief.

"Aye," said Fergie, "we did!"

The driver walked off, muttering that he didn't f-ing-well believe them.

"I still don't know 'ow we did it," Jamie spoke as if trying to convince himself, "but I know we did!"

Fergie thought for a few moments then said slowly, "I know how we got inside them; in one word."

"Wot word?"

"Fright."

8 - A train of events (September 1941)

"Come on, Charlie, let's get a move on!" Driver Jack Shaw was anxious to get his Paddington express with its seven coaches away from Birkenhead Woodside. Liverpool was getting a heavy pasting again and a few of the bombs were straying over the river. Fireman Charlie Dalrymple looked up from his checking of the gauges and glanced outside the cab to see the searchlights waving in their attempts to latch onto an enemy bomber. The guard's whistle could not be heard over the clumps of the bombs on Merseyside and so Charlie looked out along the platform to check if he could see the guard's green flag. There were still a couple of sailors hurrying along the platform and the guard was waiting with his flag to signal the right away as soon as they got into the train.

The starter signal already showed that the line was clear for the train to move out. As soon as Charlie saw the guard raise his flag, he called out to his driver and the train moved smartly off. They stopped briefly again at Rock Ferry (for passengers who preferred to escape from Liverpool via the safety of the underground Mersey Railway) to board the train and hurried away once more across the Wirral.

Just past Port Sunlight, a bomb exploded close to the track and Driver Shaw pulled up at Bromborough for an unscheduled stop, to check with the guard that there had been no damage to the train. They found three cracked windows but nothing else to report. The windows were taped over and the stationmaster told them he would phone through to Chester and get someone to thoroughly check the carriages there.

Passing Capenhurst, they caught a glimpse of an enemy bomber coming down in flames and exploding about a mile away.

"One of the fighter pilots from RAF Hooton caught one!"

called Charlie gleefully, with Jack Shaw nodding as they passed the little station at Mollington.

Thankfully, they pulled into No 2 bay at Chester General Station for the train to reverse direction. Charlie climbed down to uncouple their 2-6-2T Prairie locomotive, while at the other end of their train a 4-6-0 express passenger Castle class with four strengthening coaches backed on.

"Who's taking the train on to Wolverhampton?" Jack asked as Charlie climbed back into the cab.

"I think it's George Denton, with young Lance Hargreaves," replied Charlie. "I caught a glimpse of George as I was back on the platform."

"Hmm," commented Jack Shaw, "it's now a heavily loaded train with eleven on and a hilly run. Still, nothing that George can't handle, and young Hargreaves certainly knows which end of the shovel is which. They won't have any problems."

However, Driver Shaw's optimism was misguided; after their run from Birkenhead, the peace and quiet of the Chester location had apparently made him temporarily forget that there was a war on.

The Great Western's northern main line and the LMS north to west main lines crossed at Shrewsbury, and here their train was held up while a large number of passengers, many of them in the armed forces, changed trains. As a consequence, they were twenty minutes late in leaving. Then a platform inspector at Wellington had heard that Stafford Road shed in Wolverhampton had been bombed and mentioned to them that they could experience a problem there, too. He was right.

As they passed Stafford Road shed before pulling into Wolverhampton Low Level station, they saw evidence of bomb damage, with a few small craters around the tracks, although there didn't seem to be any major damage to any of the locomotives there. They were surprised to see a 4-6-0 King class express passenger locomotive simmering gently on one of the sidings.

"I reckon we'll be late agen 'ere, Mr D," remarked Lance as he saw the King, "I bet that's the train engine for the rest of this run to London, an' it's still on shed."

This was true: when they arrived at Wolverhampton, another large 2-6-2T Prairie tank engine added six more coaches to their train and they were approached by another inspector.

"Sorry, Driver, you'll have to take the train on to Birmingham. The Stafford Road exit tracks have been damaged and the replacement King is stuck in the shed and can't get out. You change shift at Snow Hill and a Tyseley crew will take the train on to Paddington with another Castle."

"But we've now got seventeen on, and even a King would have difficulties handling this load over the hills!" George Denton pointed out.

"Yes, I'm fully aware of that, but the best we can do is to give you our Prairie as a pilot to Snow Hill and let Tyseley deal with the train after that."

George glanced at his fireman and shook his head sorrowfully. "Sorry, Lance, you're going to be shovelling hard for the next half-hour, and there's nothing I can do about it!"

Fireman Hargreaves grinned at his driver. "Good job I et all me porridge this mornin' then, Mr D." He turned to the tender and bent to pull more coal forward. Lance was clearly not worried about having to shovel hard for a while longer.

Once the Prairie pilot engine had coupled on in front of them and the signal had cleared for them to start, Driver Denton and the pilot engine driver worked carefully to set the heavy train into motion.

"Get ready for the sanders, Lance," warned George, "she might slip with this load." A wheel-spin was a thunderous embarrassment for any driver, but the sanders were designed to send a stream of sand under the wheels, to assist with adhesion in slippery conditions. Fortunately, it wasn't raining, and the engine's wheels gripped the rails as the train moved slowly off. Half an hour later, their gradual entry into the Birmingham suburbs was depressing; as they passed the Hawthorns and Handsworth and Smethwick stations, bomb damage could frequently be seen but the two locomotives struggled on and they managed to arrive in Snow Hill Station only half an hour late.

Another Castle, with a 4-6-0 Grange general purpose engine as pilot, was waiting to take over the train for the rest of the trip to Paddington, and thankfully Driver Denton and Fireman Hargreaves were able to leave their train and run back light engine to Wolverhampton. Here, the damaged track had already been given a temporary repair and they were able to report to the Shedmaster for their return to their home shed at Chester.

Unusually, the Tyseley shed Castle was in fairly good condition, having been out of Wolverhampton Works after a general repair only three weeks previously. Furthermore, Driver Harry Symington and Fireman Roger Sinclair on the Grange had worked with Driver Pogmore and Fireman Monkton before and the four men were able to form an effective team on the two-hour run to Paddington.

There was, however, no possibility of making up lost time, as there were several signal checks, even for what in peacetime would have been a priority express. There were a couple of urgent military goods workings, which had precedence and held up the express so that by the time they were on the Paddington approaches it was already dark and they were almost two hours late.

Ian Monkton dropped from his cab to uncouple from their train and a little 0-6-0 Pannier tank coupled on at the rear, to draw the coaches out of Platform 4 and take them into the carriage sidings.

But before the Castle and the Grange could back out to the Ranelagh Road shed for turning and servicing, the air raid sirens began to wail and the first bombs could be heard, dropping in the distance.

Inside Brunel's huge Paddington train shed, waiting passengers and railway staff began hurrying towards the shelters, but before everyone was in safety a 250lb bomb hurled through the roof and scored a direct hit on a coach in a Bristol express waiting to depart from Platform 1.

Quickly, both crews from the Castle and Grange locomotives rushed round to see what they could do to assist. They were joined by the crew of another little Pannier tank, which had brought the coaches in for the express. By the time they reached the damaged coach, other staff from the station's Red Cross, as well as men from the Air Raid Precautions, were already on the scene, assisting the wounded. Ambulance bells could be heard ringing in the distance and some of the uninjured passengers who had not yet reached the shelters had returned to see if they could help.

Five of the six enginemen and the ARP men together ushered the lightly injured to the First Aid post, for nurses and a duty doctor to see to, while Roger Sinclair climbed through the end door of the bombed coach to see whether anyone was left inside. He did not get far; the centre of the coach was a shambles, and the corridor was blocked by a compartment door, which had been blown off its rail. Through the broken glass, he could see two people, neither of whom were moving, on a seat in the next compartment, so he kicked at the glass remnants in order to climb past the door without cutting himself too badly. This took a few moments and he scrambled into the compartment. Carefully checking each one, he found no obvious injuries on either but they still were not moving. He pushed his head out and called out for help.
    An ARP man came up quickly. "You orright, mate?"
    "Yeah, I'm fine. but there's two people in 'ere, an' they aren't movin' but I can't see any injuries on 'em."
    "You a passenger, was yer?"
    "No, I'm a fireman from the Birken'ead. Me and my mate are 'elpin' with the injured, an' I climbed in 'ere ter see if I could 'elp."
    "'Ow did yer get in?"
    "Through the end door."
    "Right, I'll come in that way. too."
    A moment or two later the ARP man was with him in the compartment. "Let's get these two out through the

corridor an' on to the platform so's the doc can get a look at 'em. They don't look too good ter me."

The two men eased the two people, one by one, along the corridor and onto the platform, where they laid them down gently. A nurse came up and listened while they told her what they had done. She felt for pulses but when they looked at her, she shook her head sadly. "I think they're gone," she muttered, "but we'll need a doctor to certify death formally."

By this time, the sound of bombing had ceased and more people were emerging from the shelter. A large section of the platform had been roped off. Stretchers were laid out with injured passengers on them, and these were being carried out to the waiting ambulances. A half-dozen or so bodies, covered with blankets, were also waiting to be collected, and a policeman was watching over a pile of luggage from the damaged coach.

Altogether, seven people in the coach had been killed and another seventeen badly injured.

Driver Harry Symington came up to his fireman and said, "Hey up, Roger, you've got blood all over yer trousers!"

Roger looked down in surprise. "God, so I have! I musta..." He swayed and sank, senseless, to the ground.

Harry called out to a passing nurse, "Excuse me, nurse, can you look at my mate? I think he's bleeding!"

She stopped and checked Roger's pulse and examined his leg; she snipped his trouser leg open. 'Yes," she nodded, "he's bleeding heavily; we'll get him seen to right away." She called a doctor and had Roger carried away.

At Ranelagh Road shed, one of the drivers said to Harry, "Your passengers on the Birken'ead came in wiv a bang, didn't they, 'Arry?"

"Aye," replied Harry, "and they left Merseyside with a bang, an' all. They've had a right old journey. Bombs at Merseyside and Bromborough, a downed Jerry bomber at Capenhurst, held up at Salop, bombs at Stafford Road, and then bombs when they got here. I bet it'll be a while before those passengers travel Great Western again!"

9 - UXB (March 1942)

After two and a half years of war, the British public were getting used to their new circumstances: food rationing; metal fencing removed to be used for war materials; housewives handing over their metal pots and pans for similar purposes (and then having to buy new ones to replace them). Even bombing raids were becoming an accepted part of life in London and the larger provincial cities, with most of their inhabitants prepared to hurry into cover on hearing the undulating wail of the sirens. Yet apart from the grim news from North Africa, where Rommel was running wild, there seemed to be a feeling that the Germans were no longer irresistible. The threatened invasion of Britain had not taken place and was now deemed unlikely, with the Americans as new, if untried, allies. Indeed, there was even military thought about a future counter-invasion back into France. In short, the tide, many considered, might have begun to turn.

"Ah, yes," said Driver Henry Solomon, sitting smoking his Woodbine in the enginemen's cabin in Harwich and smiling at his fireman, Trevor Redditch. "I don't mind the teak coaches; they were like that when I started on the old Great Eastern, er, except," he added, "for a short while, when they were dark red. But that didn't last; they came back to teak again. But the bigger engines looked far nicer than this apple-green we've got now."

Trevor nodded in encouragement. He liked to hear the reminiscing of his mate.

"Our dark blue engines," continued his driver, "looked spectacular until they were absorbed into the LNER and them Doncaster men made them all look like Great Northern engines."

"I heard," remarked Trevor, "that the same thing

happened to the LNWR and the Lancashire and Yorkshire. When they became the LMS, the Midland men dominated the new company and painted everything red!"

"Aye," said Henry, "that's true but I have to admit that when we got Sir Nigel Gresley from the GNR, he did build some bloody good locomotives."

"So did Stanier later in the LMS, and they pinched him from the Great Western, who stupidly let him go," continued Trevor.

The enginemen were relaxing before going on to their various shifts; Henry and Trevor were waiting to return to London, on a semi-fast passenger train in two hours' time. They had time for a break before going out to pick up their B12 4-6-0 locomotive and prepare it for the run to Liverpool Street.

"You poor devils back up to London, I take it?" asked Keith Drayton, a local driver, from Manningtree.

"Yep, that's us," replied Trevor, "but why 'poor devils'?"

"All that bombing!" explained Keith. "Me, I run local trains to Colchester, Ipswich, Felixstowe, Harwich... nice, quiet places. I once got to Norwich, even," he added thoughtfully. "Not many bombs there, either."

"Yeah, well it can get a bit rough for us," replied Trevor, "although last year was worse. We still get heavy raids in London but not quite as bad as it was. They're getting things better organised, with the shelters, warnings and so on. But don't you get bombing at Felixstowe and Harwich, being naval bases an' all?"

"Well, we did get a bad bombing raid early on but the RAF has an airfield there and they've got better fighter defences now."

One morning, Henry Solomon came into Stratford shed, the depot serving Liverpool Street, with a smirk on his face.

"What's tickling your fancy this morning, Mr S?" Trevor Redditch asked curiously. "You look like the cat that swallowed the cream."

"Wait till we're well on the road, lad," came the reply.

"I have a real treat in store for us both." And saying this, he waved a small package enticingly at his fireman. "But you'll have to hang on until it's time for a brew."

They entered the enginemen's room and studied the shift notices.

"Well, we're on the 8.30 to Yarmouth, returning on the 5.35. Should be a simple run," remarked Driver Solomon. "Let's think now," he added, "we'll have our first brew and a bit of breakfast just after Colchester, what d'you think?"

"Fine by me, Mr S," replied Trevor. "I'll definitely be a bit peckish by then; I might even be hungry enough to enjoy my dripping sandwiches."

Henry simply smiled, and Trevor wondered once more what it was that had made his driver unusually cheerful that morning.

They backed their B12 4-6-0 onto their train at Liverpool Street station and waited for the starter signal and the guard's flag. Trevor glanced at his driver to see if he could find any clue for his elevated mood, but Henry was patiently waiting for the off, without any expression on his face.

Once they were moving, Henry pointed out some of the many large and small repairs along the line, saying, "I was still a kid in the First War and although we had some shelling at Yarmouth and a few bombs from the zeppelins in London, there was nothing like this damage."

They both stared at the bombed streets, craters, repaired brickwork on tunnels and signal boxes as they passed; all evidence of the attention the East End had received from the Luftwaffe in the past two years. "They've done wonders getting all this fixed up again so quickly so that the trains can go through," continued Henry.

As they hurried through Ilford and Brentwood, the damage was less obvious, although the scene was still depressing, emphasised by the rain which had started to come down. Their first stop was at Shenfield, where the branches to Southend and Burnham-on-Crouch left the main line, and Trevor took the opportunity to climb on the tender with the coal hammer and break up some big lumps so that they would pass easily into the firebox.

Henry nodded in approval. "Good lad, we don't want to be held up by a lump of coal jamming the firehole."

Trevor wondered at this comment, for no competent fireman missed the chance of avoiding future problems while the engine was at a standstill. It made balancing on the coal easier and the hammering more accurate, and also avoided the risk of being hit by a tunnel mouth. He knew that his driver regarded him as efficient, so the remark appeared to be superfluous and Driver Solomon was not a man who wasted words. All very puzzling. Why was the man so cheerful?

After they left Colchester, they were coasting smoothly along. Henry took his tea bag from the shelf and said, "Time for a brew." Trevor flattened a spot in the firebox for their jerry can of water to boil quickly while Henry poured the tea-leaves into the water.

"Right, young Trevor, clean your shovel, we're having a bacon sandwich each," he said as he unwrapped four slices of bread and two rashers of bacon.

Trevor stared in astonishment. "Bacon?" he gasped. "But Mr S, your bacon ration is for you and your missus; you don't need to share it with me."

"You don't want any?" said Henry with a grin, "Well in that case..."

"No, of course not; I didn't say that!" responded Trevor hurriedly.

"Only joking; you're a good fireman, Trevor, and this is just to say thanks. And my missus agrees, but I can't promise to make a habit of it."

Four minutes later, Henry handed his fireman the first sandwich. "There you go, put that down your gullet."

Trevor sat down gratefully for the first time since they had left Liverpool Street, sinking his teeth into the treat; chewing with his eyes closed in bliss, while Henry popped the second rasher on the shovel.

At this moment, Trevor noticed a darkening of the fire, due to some dubious coal, and, without thinking, he stepped up and put the blower on to increase the firebox draught, so raising the temperature of the fire and maintaining pressure; the reaction was instinctive, yet highly unfortunate in the circumstances. The sizzling bacon on the shovel instantly disappeared into the flames, to the shout of despair from his driver.

It was shortly before they reached Ipswich Docks, and not before a lot of hard work with the pricker to unclog the grate, that peace reigned once more between the two crewmen. But any feeling that either may have had that the rest of the run was now going to be easier was quickly dispersed by the sight of the next home signal at danger. Up until this point – and in spite of the bacon disaster – they had been running on time, but it seemed that a delay was about to occur.

They pulled up at the home signal and waited for it to clear but there appeared to be a group of men next to the line as they waited. One of the men in the field a few yards from one of their carriages shouted something which neither crewman understood and they saw a policeman hurry over to him. The first man was standing still, looking at something in the grass near some cattle.

"Get the farmer quickly, 'e'll have to drive 'is cows away!" the policeman called urgently when he saw what the man was staring at. "There's a bloody bomb sittin' 'ere wot 'asn't gone orf!"

Shortly, a man with a dog hurried over to the cattle and began to chivvy them away. The policeman shouted for someone to telephone the army for an explosive expert to come and sort out the problem. By this time, a railway official had arrived. He came to look at the bomb, turned and walked over to the locomotive, and climbed into the cab.

"Did you catch all that, Driver?" he asked.

"Yes I think so," replied Henry. "It sounded like they've found an unexploded bomb right next to the train."

"Yes, they have. I'm afraid you can't move until the bomb disposal people come and let us know whether it's safe. In the meantime, I'll let the guard know that everybody is to leave the train without their luggage; they must get out on the far side. We can't have passengers wandering around. Oh," he added, "and on no account must any door be allowed to slam shut."

Twenty minutes later, an army officer arrived and examined the bomb carefully. He sent all the other men away to a safe distance and then came over to speak to the railway official. "I'm afraid this is a delicate and serious situation. I'm grateful that you have got all your passengers away safely."

"Can I move our train away down the track?" asked Henry.

"Definitely not," answered the officer, emphatically. "The wheel vibrations of a moving train could very easily trigger the fuse." He returned to the bomb and sent his assistant with an unravelling wire to a safer distance, where the latter could wait behind a tree trunk. The officer then set out his instruments on a cloth and began to feel his way round the bomb.

The four railwaymen, having seen the passengers to safety, followed, leaving the train standing quietly with all brakes on and the fire dampened down. Three railwaymen walked to the nearest station, which was half a mile away, to wait in safety until the bomb was taken away, leaving Henry to check that all was safe in the engine before he too could get to safety. Then Henry, Trevor and their guard watched from a distance until they could return to their train and bring it to the station for the passengers, and continue on their journey.

A young soldier was explaining the bomb removal procedure to them: "The UXB officer, the Unexploded Bomb Officer," he added, "with the bomb, is in phone contact with his assistant, who is sitting a safe distance away, and he explains what he is doing as he works so that if, well, if the worst happens, then the assistant will know exactly what the officer was doing when it blew. This is useful informa—"

At that moment, there was a loud explosion and they all saw the cloud of smoke and debris as part of one of the carriages disintegrated, alongside where the bomb had been.

"Christ!" muttered the young soldier. "Poor sod. Lieutenant Benson was a good bloke to work with. He's the third officer in our unit to be lost since August."

Driver Solomon looked at his fireman. "Just think, Trev, what if that bomb had gone off while we were passing!"

"Doesn't bear thinking about! I'm bloody glad I work for the railway and not the army."

The breakdown train came early the next morning to remove the wreckage of the coach and to repair the track, which had been damaged. The line was functioning again two days later.

10 - A tiny railway declares war (April 1942)

Geoffrey Bilston was not one of the more successful students at Taunton Grammar School; he had a pleasant and somewhat appealing personality, and was not particularly lazy, but neither was he overly ambitious. He was quite happy to bumble along, taking whatever life had to give him without complaint. He left school at the age of fifteen, and was working as a general dogsbody in a grocery store in Taunton, using what little money he earned by paying his mother five shillings a week for his keep and, if possible, putting a little something aside occasionally to be able to buy a second-hand addition to his Hornby train set. New items were no longer available, as Meccano Ltd of Binns Rd, Liverpool, were fully involved with war work.

When war broke out, Geoffrey was called up to join the army, receiving basic training and being assessed for any special skills to be trained in.

"What d'you reckon to Private Bilston, Sergeant?" asked the Lieutenant in charge of allotting the recruits at the end of their basic training.

"Hard to say, sir, the PBI might be his best bet."

The PBI, or 'Poor Bloody Infantry', was the backbone of the army, into which most soldiers were sent before they became specialists of one sort or another. The officer nodded and added Geoffrey's name to the long list recommended for the Somerset Light Infantry.

Some weeks later, Geoffrey found himself on route marches, firing ranges, kitchen duties, unarmed combat exercises, and all the usual round of infantry training. He showed no affinity for any other specialist skills and appeared, therefore, to be ideal for the general duties of the infantry. But even here, he was too placid to show any aggression in shooting or bayonet work. Indeed, the only real interest he showed was when he heard that the Somerset Light Infantry had a unit responsible for looking after the little Romney, Hythe and Dymchurch fifteen-inch gauge enthusiasts' railway, which had been taken over by the War Office. It had been originally built by Captain Jack Howey in 1927 and Geoffrey had once visited the railway and been quite charmed by it. Aside from this, he was quite prepared to go along with what life served up, without any major exertions on his part. What he did not know was that life had rather more active plans for him...

On completion of his basic training, he applied for a posting to this railway, and was surprised to find he was accepted. Within a month, Private Bilston reported to the officer commanding the unit at New Romney. He was told to wait outside until he was called so he spent some time admiring the special armoured train, which had been built in 1940 to help protect the line; one of the line's large engines had been armour-plated and two high-sided wagons had been constructed for it. These wagons each held two Lewis machine guns and an anti-tank rifle, along with the teams to manage them. As he was staring at the locomotive, a soldier leaned out of the cab. "Like the engine then, do yer, mate?"

"Which one is she?"

"I dunno mate, I only driver 'er."

"She's a 4-8-2; the line's only got two of them: No 5 *Hercules*, and No 6 *Samson*."

"*Hercules*, I think; she does the job but she clanks a bit. She was built in 1927."

"Clanks?" Geoffrey looked at the coupling rods. "P'raps the motion needs checking for looseness?" He remembered that his own pre-war Hornby 4-4-0 *County of Bedford* had rattled a little; a problem which he traced to a loose rivet on the connecting rod.

"Like I said, I only drive 'er."

Geoffrey stooped to look closely at the engine; it was one-third the size of a 'real' locomotive, and stood some four-foot-six inches high. He examined the coupling and connecting rods, which were visible, wondering why this vulnerable motion had not been plated over.

"What brings you here, Private Bilston?" enquired Lieutenant Savage of the newcomer before him.

"Er – interest, sir. I like trains, and—"

"Ah, I see. Come to play on our toy trains, have you?"

Geoffrey didn't know how to answer this so kept quiet.

"What shooting experience have you?"

"Basic training, sir."

"Basic only? Good god, man, we need trained machine gunners – ever fired a machine gun?"

"Only a Bren once, sir."

There was a knock at the door.

"Enter," called Savage.

A soldier entered snapped to attention and saluted. "Problem with the armoured engine, sir."

"A problem?"

"Loose alignment in the crosshead, sir."

"Very impressive, Private Clissold. Anyway, how do you know that?"

"This new squaddie 'ere, sir," the soldier pointed at Geoff. "'E mentioned it 'alf an hour ago an' I got a fitter to check it, an' 'e found the problem. 'E ses 'e can fix it by termorrer, sir."

"Hmm," said the officer, eyeing Geoffrey once more. "Perhaps we can use you, after all. But you'll need extra training."

Three months later, Private Bilston was sitting in the armoured train on patrol along the coast, behind his Lewis gun. The loader was next to him and the third man of the team sat on his left, ready to clear any jams or water cooling difficulties. The second team sat near them with an anti-tank rifle team on the other side; the second wagon was behind the engine. They were waiting behind some bushes, watching for low-flying raiders sneaking in under the radar from the sea, when the observer with his binoculars called out, "'Ere we are, lads! Three Focke-Wulfs comin' low at ten o'clock!"

Instantly, four machine guns swung round to the left and took aim as the raiders swept in, less than half a mile from the train. All guns blasted away and one of the raiders blew up as they crossed the beach.

"Yer got one, Geoff, yer jammy sod!" chortled Fred Cooper, his loader, amid joyful shouts from the other teams as well. "On yer first duty, an' all!"

It was a jubilant train that steamed into their depot that day.

The following Saturday, a dance had been arranged for the troops, and nurses from a local hospital had been invited. Geoffrey had always been unsure of himself around girls and stood back until a pretty, dark-haired nurse with striking blue eyes came over to him.

"Not dancing tonight, soldier?" she asked.

"Errm, er, I don't dance very well," he muttered.

"Time you learned, then. Come on." She grabbed his arm and led him onto the dance floor. He danced with her several times that night and by the end of the evening he was in love.

"Yer got one agen, Geoff, yer lucky bugger!" chuckled Fred Cooper on their way back to the barracks. "An' the best o' the bunch!"

From then on, whenever both were off duty, Nurse Robotham and Private Bilston spent their free time together. One very pleasant afternoon, they had cycled to a secluded spot near the beach, a mile or two from Dungeness, with the intention of taking a dip in a creek. They could not go to the beach, due to the barbed wire entanglements, tank traps, and other hindrances to a potential invasion.

Geoffrey was in his swimming trunks, lying in the sun, when Jenny came out of the little creek. He stared at her, observing the way that her bathing costume emphasised her well-developed figure; wondering whether the shoulder straps were loose enough for him to slip his hand down her back, or even – a thrilling idea – down her front. When she knelt down and kissed him, her kiss brought about a conspicuous problem in his trunks, and before he could turn over on his stomach to hide the difficulty, she saw his red face then noticed the incriminating bulge.

"Don't be embarrassed, Geoff," she smiled. "I'm very flattered!" She put her hand on his chest, pushed him down and kissed him again. Geoff's discomfort eased slightly then turned to turmoil as he felt her hand slide down his belly and inside his bathers. A few moments later, she withdrew her hand, patted him on the stomach and remarked, "There you go, soldier, problem solved!"

Over the next five months, Geoff was coached discreetly among bushes on Romney Marsh, with more advanced training on the many ways the human body could experience intense pleasure. This continued until Nurse Robotham's transfer to a hospital near Leicester, leaving behind a disconsolate private soldier.

Meanwhile, on the tiny armoured train he had achieved another possible hit on a raid; this time a Stuka, which banked after taking a line of bullet holes across the rear fuselage, turned out to sea and headed back, smoking, across the Channel.

In early 1943, patrolling with the armoured train was usually a boring duty as they rarely saw action, and Geoffrey, now a lance-corporal, tried to conquer his boredom by assisting the fitters in the shed when rolling stock was being repaired.

One afternoon, he was on one of the ballast trains when a bomb hit the track in front of the train, without blowing up. The bomb bounced once then exploded sixty yards further on, covering the train with grass and mud. Lieutenant Savage, travelling in an open wagon, came forward to see whether the driver had been injured. He had suffered a severe fright and, although he wasn't physically hurt, he could not stop shaking.

"Come along, Private Johnson, get the train moving again," the officer said curtly.

"I c-c-can't, sir," replied the shocked driver. "Me hands won't stop shakin'." He appeared to be totally incapable of coherent action.

"Pull yourself together, man!" commanded Savage. "And

look at the disgraceful condition of your engine!"

"*What!*"

"Your engine, Johnson! It's covered in filth. How can you allow it to look like this?"

"B-but that's not my fault, sir, the bomb—"

"You will spend your rest afternoon in the shed, cleaning that engine. Now get this train moving again!"

Private Johnson was almost incandescent with fury as he eased himself down into his cab and seized the controls. As the train moved slowly off again, Geoffrey shot a look of admiration at Lieutenant Savage; the officer had cured Johnson's terror by converting it to anger.

One late afternoon, Geoffrey was working on one of the engines in the locomotive shed at New Romney, when the sirens sounded. Before he could leave for the shelter, a bomb landed twenty yards away. The wall was blasted open and two of the engines suffered considerable damage. Luckily, their bulk protected Geoffrey from fatal injury, but he was hospitalised for several weeks. After his return to light duties, a number of Women's Land Army girls arrived in Hythe to work on local farms. Geoffrey now found reciprocal interest in his sexual proclivities, although the vigorous enthusiasm of one of the girls seriously threatened his 'light duties' status. She later moved to Devon, bearing his unwitting gift in her belly.

Early in the new year, the railway was involved in moving heavy materials along the coast, in preparation for the planned invasion of France and the armoured train, occasionally with Lance-Corporal Bilston driving, was in demand to watch for hit-and-run attacks by raiders trying to disrupt Allied invasion plans. One week, there were three low-level attacks, and Geoffrey succeeded in shooting down another aircraft, which led to a promotion to full Corporal, and a medal.

On Geoffrey's demobilisation in August 1945, the RH&DR acquired a highly competent mechanic and part-time driver, and Mrs Carol Bilston, late of the Women's Land

Army, had gained a husband and two children. Geoffrey's contribution to the nation's war effort was two – possibly three – downed enemy aircraft and three children, although he was admittedly unaware of one of the latter.

11 - The Troops are not amused (August 1942)

Driver Ken Snowdon and his fireman Jem Willis were struggling with their Hall class 4-6-0 mixed traffic locomotive to haul their Empty Coaching Stock of ten corridors up Gresford Bank on their way to Wrexham. This should have been a straightforward run, with a Hall in good nick, but their engine was due for some maintenance and wasn't steaming at all well.

As they passed over the crest at little more than jogging pace, Ken turned to his fireman: "We could be in for some trouble at Wrexham when the squaddies board the train, Jem. If she's not pulling well now, what will she be like when we have passengers?"

Their train was a troop train, due to take some 300 troops south to Salisbury for further training. But at an army training base some miles away, the squaddies were also unhappy. Regimental Sergeant-Major Geoffrey Clamp sighed as he caught sight of the new Second Lieutenant heading towards his company. The young officer was straight out of school – Eton, as it chanced - and into the Officers Training Corps, and had been sent on completion of his training to the South Cheshires.

"Just look after him, Geoff," murmured the Major. "He's still wet behind the ears and won't know his boots from his bayonet."

"Yessir," replied the RSM. "'E's in charge of 3rd Platoon of new recruits, but I've put Sarn't Kemp in charge of 'em. "'E'll keep a weather eye on 'is new officer."

"Very good; but let me know in a couple of weeks how he's making out with his men."

Second Lieutenant Andrew Benbow had done well at school and had intended to go to Oxford but the army had claimed him, deciding he was officer material and sending him for training. He was a little apprehensive at being told he was to be in charge of a platoon of about thirty soldiers, and had been advised to heed the advice of his platoon sergeant. Their infantry training was to be on Salisbury Plain, where they were headed once they had boarded the train at Wrexham.

At Wrexham General, Driver Ken Snowdon in the cab watched as 150 troops were waiting to board his train. He turned to his fireman. "Look at them, Jem, wouldn't you like to be a squaddy as well? No oil on yer clothes, no shovelling four tons of coal a day; no watching gauges; no gettin' wet in the rain an' no goin' to work at four in the morning?"

Fireman Jeremy Freeman chuckled, "An' no gettin' shot at day or night; no mate, I'm happy where I am, ta."

"You might change your mind by the time we reach Salisbury. We're now well loaded; I reckon you'll 'ave shovelled six ton today!"

Outside Wrexham General Station, the platoon were standing at ease as a truck pulled up and a group of officers jumped out.

"Look at that!" an indignant call echoed from the ranks. "We've 'ad ter march five mile, and the bloody officers get ter ride in a truck!" RSM Clamp met Second Lieutenant Benbow and pointed out his platoon. Andrew Benbow marched over to them.

"Oh Gawd, another bloody useless officer fer us!" muttered Trooper Bennett as 2nd Lt. Benbow joined them. "E's only just out o' nappies!"

Trooper Mercer's *sotto voce* comment was nevertheless heard by most of the company, "'Ow will 'e know wot orders ter give?"

An hour later, as the train paused in Shrewsbury for further troops to board, Jeremy heard an announcer's voice as a down express slowly rolled into the opposite platform. *"The train arriving on Platform Two is for Birkenhead, calling at Ruabon, Wrexham, Chester, Hooton, Rock Ferry and Birkenhead Woodside."*

"I wonder how many of the squaddies will ever hear that again," Jem remarked to Ken Snowdon, "if they're headed for North Africa."

But Fireman Willis had other, more pressing, worries of his own. The train was heavily loaded by now and the right-hand cylinder gland of their Hall was leaking badly. He also suspected that the smokebox ash hadn't been properly emptied, thus hindering their steaming. By the time they had reached Bristol, he was exhausted. He had a brief opportunity to recover while they uncoupled and ran to the coaling tower at St Philips' Marsh shed for more coal and water, before coupling up again to their train, but even though his driver had taken the shovel a couple of times, he knew there was to be no relief until they reached Salisbury; crew rosters in wartime were often very demanding. But for the 200 troops, the lunch parcels expected to be delivered at Shrewsbury were not available; there had been a communication breakdown between army caterers, and the squaddies went hungry until they arrived in Bristol, where only a meagre supply was handed out.

There was some light relief as they were held up at signals near Westbury and they could observe the antics of a lovesick bull as it tried to persuade a reluctant cow to allow him to have his way with her. She was big enough to discourage him time and time again and finally the bull lumbered away, frustrated and unfulfilled.

"Reminds me of a bird I met in Liverpool on me last leave," remarked Trooper Braithwaite, " I tried 'ard ter get me end away but she weren't 'avin' any."

Just after they were beginning to pick up speed after the signal check, Second Lieutenant Benbow glanced out of the window, stared into the sky and then hurried to urgently find his sergeant.

"Who's got the best eyesight in the platoon, Sergeant?" he asked.

"That'd be Trooper Standish, sir, 'e's a sniper."

"Well, get him to have a look at those two aircraft, high

up over on the right."

Trooper Standish looked carefully at the aircraft pointed out to him and then said, "I think they're Jerries, sir, they look like Stukas."

The two aircraft began to make a wide turn. "You're right, Trooper Standish," said Benbow quickly, "I can now see the black crosses on their wings, and I think they are looking for a target of opportunity, which we might be supplying them. A troop train would be a dream target, although they won't know that this train is one!"

As he spoke, the signal dropped and the train began to move off. Benbow knew that a train was helpless against dive-bombing, unless the driver could vary his speed rapidly to avoid an attack. He also knew that the one weakness for a Stuka pilot was that once he began his dive he was committed and could not change his angle of attack.

The bomber tilted sideways and began its dive towards the train. Second Lieutenant Benbow waited for a few seconds until the Stuka pilot was committed and then he reached up and yanked the emergency communication cord. The train instantly lurched and began to slow down, jerking several soldiers in the corridor off their feet.

"What'd the stupid sod do that for?" yelled a trooper as he rubbed his injured behind after falling to the floor, "'E'll 'ave us all in 'orspital!"

"Hold tight, lads!" yelled Benbow. "There could be a crash!"

But the slowing train had avoided the bomb the Stuka had released and it landed close to the track some eighty yards ahead. The tracks had been damaged and, as the train screeched to a halt beside the crater, the locomotive derailed and the first two coaches followed it, the first listing to one side.

The 3rd Platoon were further back and their coach was undamaged but there were cries of pain and alarm from the front of the train. "Get our men out into the field, Sergeant," called Benbow urgently. "The second plane may come and attack as well. We should get a machine gun and the sniper ready if possible."

"Right you are, sir," answered Sergeant Kemp, smartly.

"It's worth a try and it might put the second bugger off his aim!" He ordered the platoon out and had Trooper Standish with his sniper rifle ready. The platoon had two Bren gunners loading their Brens and other platoons had begun to organise themselves as well. The second Stuka pilot could see the hastily assembled rifle and machine gun troops as he began his dive on the train and curved away, pulling out early still high enough for no serious damage to be inflicted on his aircraft.

However, the lead Stuka had already done serious damage and the derailed part of the train contained a good many men, whose injuries ranged from minor to serious. These were quickly examined by the medical staff, who very fortunately had been in the rear of the train and were relatively unharmed, aside from bruising they had suffered when the emergency brakes had been applied.

Both crewmen had been injured and their engine had been damaged by the derailment, and had bent a connecting rod. Clearly, the rest of the journey would have to be by road and it would be some time before road transport could be organised. By the time the lorries finally arrived, their evening sandwiches had become stale, tasteless and almost inedible.

Sergeant Kemp's platoon, who had been badly shaken about, were not happy. "That new sprog officer pulled the bloody communication cord and knocked us all arse over tit, Sarn't!" complained one trooper.

Sergeant Kemp too was not too pleased, either; he had hoped for better in his new officer and had not heard Andrew Benbow's warning. He growled at his platoon and told them to tone down their language, attempting to defend his officer, but they knew that he was also unhappy with the situation.

Arriving very late in Salisbury, the troops were formed up to board more lorries, to be taken to their billets. At the training ground, the troops found tents ready, rather than the huts they had hoped for.

"We're goin' to bloody freeze tonight!" grumbled Trooper Braithwaite as the 3rd Platoon made their way to their tents. "Why couldn't that young sod keep 'is 'ands to 'isself? First he pulls the bloody cord an' then 'e 'auls us all outside to shoot at that Jerry plane wot we can't 'it wiv our popguns!"

There was a good deal of grumbling that evening among the soldiers of the platoon. But Trooper Braithwaite was in for a surprise. Their Regimental Sergeant-Major himself called the platoon together. "You'll all be pleased to know that the engine driver an' 'is fireman are in hospital and not badly hurt;" he began. "And aren't you the lucky ones? How many of you are still fit to fight after the attack?"

Sergeant Kemp looked round the platoon. "We're all fit, sir," he replied. "Only a couple of minor injuries. Why?"

"Tell me, Sergeant Kemp; how many of you would have been fit if the train had been hit by that bomb, and then the second Jerry had come down and attacked?"

Sgt Kemp hesitated, "Er – I should think we'd all' ave been in the shit, sir."

"You would an' all. And do you know why that bomb missed us? And why that second Jerry didn't attack?"

"No, sir. Why?"

"Because your platoon is lucky, Sergeant, that's why."

"How's that, sir?"

By this time, the troops in the platoon were all listening attentively.

"You've got a new sprog officer, and he's a clever bugger. He slowed the train in time to miss the bomb, and then he had you lot out and firing at the second aircraft."

"Cor blimey!" Trooper Braithwaite gasped out his surprise, and there were similar expressions from other soldiers. But there was a surprise for RSM Clamp, too; he had not noticed Andrew Benbow right behind him as he was talking to the platoon.

"Thank you, RSM," remarked Second Lieutenant Benbow, smiling as the RSM turned round to stare at the young officer in acute embarrassment. "It's nice to know I'm a clever bugger!"

12 - An engine bites back! (September 1942)

The Allies were in serious trouble: although America had joined Britain in the war, their troops had as yet had little chance to make their presence felt. They were still being ferried across the Atlantic, using the great passenger liners. The *Queen Mary* and *Queen Elizabeth* were making journeys from the USA, chock-full of American soldiers. Their routes were kept secret and their high speed was such that they had so far avoided the U-boat attacks, which had been so devastating to the convoys during 1941; a time the U-boat captains were describing as the 'Happy time'. Now that American ships were assisting in defending the Atlantic convoys, the Royal Navy was no longer doing the job on its own and could give more attention to dealing with the German U-boat menace.

On land, however, things were less promising: Rommel with his Afrika Korps was making a major nuisance of himself and had driven the British Eighth army back along the North African coast to the gates of Cairo itself. If he could reach the Suez Canal, he could cut off Britain's oil supplies, and that didn't bear thinking about; not, perhaps, the best time for Churchill to give the army a new commander. But Bernard Montgomery was an unusual commander.

Back at home, air raids were still occurring across most of the country, but at least RAF Bomber Command was beginning to hit back with vigour. On one night in May, a thousand bombers had hit and devastated Cologne. Hitler had earlier boasted of his new architectural designs and claimed his people would soon be unable to recognise their own cities. They were beginning to see the irony.

However, the Germans weren't the only people to see a change in their affairs. Driver Derek 'Deg' Morton sighed as he backed his elderly E2 0-6-0T tank engine onto its short Empty Coaching Stock train at East Grinstead, ready to take it on to Lancing on the south coast, where the three coaches were due for refurbishment. They ought to have been withdrawn and scrapped years earlier but the demands of wartime service had kept much rolling stock and many locomotives in service long after they were due for replacement. The coaches' refurbishment would in any case only be to keep them safe in service; it would do little for their appearance. Whereas in previous years, Lancing had sent repaired coaches looking like new, any paint they received now would only be to protect the outer surface; they would come out clearly patched. But it wasn't only the coaches which needed replacing; Driver Morton's engine needed some minor attention from the fitters. Still, he knew there was little point in suggesting this to his shed foreman. The man would be sympathetic but it was unlikely that anything would actually be done until the issue was critical, and possibly not even then. The Southern repair shops at Eastleigh were far too occupied with more urgent work. "You'll have to soldier on like the rest of us," was a common response to such requests.

Driver Morton looked across to his fireman young, James Allport, known to one and all as 'Jumping Jimmy', due to his habit of eagerly leaping into any duty to which he was assigned. In spite of his years of firing, he still hadn't lost his basic enthusiasm for his work on the Southern Railway, and was always eager to learn as much as he could from his experienced driver.

Three years of increasingly difficult wartime service had many railwaymen yearning for the previous peacetime days of adequate food, manageable hours of work and relatively clean rolling stock. These days, eight-hour shifts could often stretch to twelve or fifteen, and twenty hours was not unknown. Food was strictly rationed and clean rolling stock but a distant memory. Still, none of this dampened Jimmy's enthusiasm. He was ever an optimist. Derek

Morton felt that he was fortunate to have such a competent youngster for his regular fireman and Jumping Jimmy was equally thankful whenever he found himself on duty with Driver Morton.

Nevertheless, on a pleasant and mild autumn day in early September, Derek Morton was not a happy man. His day had begun poorly; his wife had been unable to provide his egg for breakfast as she had used up their last egg on a failed (and barely edible) cake and he had to make do with porridge, which he disliked. The butcher had run out of chops the previous Friday and only poor quality mince was available. In his lunch box were only bread-and-dripping sandwiches and a bottle of cold tea. His thermos flask had broken when it fell off the footplate and there were none left in the shops. To cap the day off, Driver Morton had forgotten to clean his boots and he detested having to come on duty in dirty boots, even though most enginemen rarely bothered about such details.

But Fireman Allport was all smiles as he joined his driver in the messroom.

Derek Morton looked up as Jumping Jimmy entered. "What are you grinning about?" he asked sourly.

"Only three coaches to Lancing?" beamed Jimmy, "Doddle of a job, and look 'ere," he said, opening his lunch box and showing the contents to his mate, "real 'am on me sandwiches! Me mam got some yesterday from Auntie Marion's farm. Aunt Marion is me mam's sister."

"Gawd, yer jammy sod!" grumbled Derek, enviously thinking of his bread and dripping.

"We sometimes even get a bit o' pork an' all," continued Jimmy, oblivious to his mate's poor mood; "an' we can share them 'am sandwiches when we 'ave our tea break."

The thought of getting his teeth into a spot of ham made Derek's mouth water and improved his mood rapidly. He hadn't tasted ham for so long that he'd almost forgotten what a pleasure it was.

Once more, he was thankful for the cheerful young mate he was blessed with. In a better frame of mind, he led the way to their locomotive and climbed into the cab, while

Jimmy collected the oil and sundry other tools from the stores clerk.

They backed onto their three coaches, which were scheduled to run as Empty Coaching Stock to Lancing via Lewes, meaning that they didn't have to go into a platform at East Grinstead to pick up any passengers. As there was no urgency, they expected to be held up in at least one or two refuges, for more important trains to be able to pass them.

The first part of their shift passed slowly and sedately, with only one five-minute worry as a pair of Messerschmidt fighters passed them high overhead, but they were heading north and paid no attention to the train, for which the enginemen were thankful. Low-altitude attacks were one of the hazards and all Southern railwaymen kept a careful eye open when they were near the coast. Especially along the coastal strip; enemy aircraft sometimes flew just above the waves, thus avoiding the radar, to drop their bombs without warning on coastal targets.

Just past Hove, near the beach, they were signalled into another refuge, to allow a fast freight to Portsmouth to pass. The pause was long enough to allow a brew-up and here Jumping Jimmy opened his lunchbox, under the eager gaze of his driver, and divvied out the sandwiches. Derek took out his own bread-and-dripping sandwiches and ate them before placing the two ham sandwiches from Jimmy into his box, explaining, "I'll keep these for later." He relished the thought of having that ham later in the afternoon. The box was carefully stowed away on the shelf in front of the coal bunker.

Unfortunately, the crew of the passing Portsmouth freight were having trouble. Their N class 2-6-0 was in poor shape and obviously needed attention from the fitters; it was leaking smoke and steam from a variety of places and was very slow, which meant that Derek and Jimmy were also held up in their refuge as the freight moved through the section. As soon as the main line was clear, they looked to their own signal for permission to leave the refuge siding, but this did not happen. The main line was signalled for a local passenger train to pass and they were held for another ten minutes.

"It's because we're only ECS," grumbled Derek. "We're not on revenue service so we're at the bottom of the list."

"We could have another brew-up then, Mr M, and you can get into your ham sandwiches," suggested Jumping Jimmy with a grin.

The local passenger passed them but before they were signalled back onto the main line another train was signalled through, holding them up again.

"Would you believe it!" There was distinct impatience in Driver Morton's voice this time. "I think we will have another brew." Jimmy quickly prepared the tea billy and put tea leaves in.

"And I think I'll sample your ham sandw—" Driver Morton stopped suddenly, staring out to sea. A dot just above the sea level had appeared, heading their way. He stared for a moment as the dot grew larger and took on the shape of an approaching German fighter aircraft. "Jimmy! Off the cab and get your head down. I think this is a hit-and-run raid, and we're the target!" He grabbed his fireman and shoved him to the steps then clambered down off the cab himself. Both men hurried away from the engine, dropped down flat in the field forty yards away, and watched. The aircraft swooped lower, at high speed, flying less than twenty feet overhead. At a hundred yards away, the pilot opened fire on their engine, sending its cannon shells straight through the boiler. Immediately, the locomotive boiler exploded, sending shards of metal and a cloud of smoke in all directions as the aircraft flew right over it.

They caught a glimpse of the pilot's smiling face through the Perspex cab as he passed them but his pleasure at his success was short-lived: his stricken aircraft dipped and crashed into the field a hundred yards further on, bursting instantly into a fireball. Perhaps a piece of the locomotive boiler had hit the aircraft's engine, or part of the ailerons on the wing or tailfin; or possibly the smoke had blinded the pilot, who then couldn't see where he was flying. Either way, there was no chance of his survival. The aircraft had been near the beginning of its patrol and had had an almost full fuel tank, resulting in the spectacular crash.

It wasn't long before a number of police appeared with railwaymen trying hard to deter arriving spectators, eager to try and grab souvenirs and risk their lives in doing so.

One of the policemen came over to check on the two shaken crewmen. "Were you the crew of that engine, lads?" he asked. "And are either of you hurt at all? Shall we call for an ambulance?"

"No, Officer," replied Jimmy excitedly, "but we had a splendid view of that Jerry going into the ground! He fired at us, but our old engine made mincemeat of him!"

"And you, Driver," said the policeman turning to Driver Morton. "Are you injured at all?"

"No," said Derek Morton, "but I'm very angry!"

"Angry?" The policeman was startled, "Why? You've apparently shot down an enemy aircraft; what on earth have you got to be angry about?"

Derek pointed furiously at the burning aircraft wreckage. "That sodding German destroyed my ham sandwiches!"

13 - A railwayman's dilemma (February 1943)

Shunter Fred Boughton stared at the rake of green Southern Railway coaches marshalled along a siding at Southampton docks. Every coach had three soldiers standing by each door; they were waiting for the passengers, who were slowly disembarking from the troopship tied up at the dockside. He shook his head sadly at the sight of the troops; they were German Army POWs and were headed for a prison camp in the north. Although their uniforms were dilapidated and torn, some were without their headgear and they shuffled down the gangplanks, once they were lined up on the quayside with their NCOs checking that their lines were straight, their discipline reasserted itself.

Fred had seen many German POWs on the dockside, men of the German Army who were so shocked by their defeat by soldiers supposedly their inferiors that they had lost all self-respect. But today's troops were different; they were Rommel's Afrika Korps and they had fought hard, and been defeated by superior numbers, and by their own totally inadequate support. Many had found the Allies' Eighth Army to be their equal in fighting ability and that the American troops, new and inexperienced though they were, lacked nothing in bravery and determination. Nevertheless, these troops stood proud and unashamed: aware of what they had achieved. Rommel had refused to accept any of the brutality that the Wehrmacht had exhibited elsewhere, and both sides in North Africa had treated their enemies with respect.

Fred had seen it all before. He had fought in the Great War and been wounded, captured and well-treated. He had even learned a good deal of German in his two years of captivity and had no hatred of these men, believing that most of them, like his own Great War comrades, were just squaddies following orders.

As the Wehrmacht men were being entrained by their own NCOs, watched diligently by their British guards, a King Arthur class 4-6-0 locomotive backed slowly on to the long troop train and Fred moved to couple the engine to it. One of the guards moved to the edge of the platform to watch him couple up the coaches to the tender. He then leaned over to offer Fred a hand to climb up onto the platform.

"Ta mate," said Fred. "These fellas give you any trouble?"

"Nah," replied the guard. "These blokes seem decent enough and they do what yer tell 'em without bellyachin'. Mind you," he added "couple of months back we 'ad some Waffen SS troops on a POW train. They was arrogant sods an' needed careful watchin'. One of 'em spoke some English and gave me a bit o' lip." The Waffen SS were Nazi hard-core soldiers, generally detested by the regular German troops.

"What did you do?" asked Fred curiously.

"I told' im ter shut 'is cake 'ole, an' as I turned to go, me rifle swung round off me shoulder and 'it 'im in the mug, accidental like. Shut 'im up smartish."

"I bet it did!" Fred laughed.

As they were chatting, Fireman Joe Bixley from the locomotive climbed down to join them. "Mornin' Fred, an' how are we this bright mornin'?" he said breezily. "All coupled up?"

"Sure, Joe, ready for the off, soon as the boards are off for you."

"You the fireman?" asked the guard, addressing Joe.

"Yep, that's me," replied Joe. "Why?"

"Oh nuthin'; taken a POW train before, 'ave yer?"

"Yeah, several times. Why?"

"'Ow is it different from an ordinary train?"

"Not a lot, really. We usually just have a quiet run and don't stop too much in the usual places. Today, for instance, we go as far as Basingstoke on our Southern main line, then we take the GWR up to Reading. Here, the train reverses, so we hand the train over to a GWR engine and crew, and they take it on through Banbury and Birmingham, on to a camp near Shifnal. You expecting any bother?"

"Nah, this lot'll be quiet, you should 'ave an easy run."

"Well, that's nice to know." Joe nodded as the guard shouldered his rifle, moved off and climbed into the train.

"What kept you, Joe?" asked Les Harriman, his driver, as he climbed back into the cab.

"I was talking to Fred the shunter and one of the army guards came to chat as well, Les."

"What did he have to say?"

"He was saying that these POWs were a quiet lot and we shouldn't expect any trouble from them."

"Trouble?" Les was surprised. "Why would we have trouble? It's the army's job to look after the POWs, we only drive the train."

But just then, Joe heard the train guard's whistle and glanced out of the cab down the platform. "There's the off, Les."

Driver Harriman sounded the whistle and he eased the locomotive gently away from the terminus. But Driver Harriman's hope of having no problems was to fail.

As they passed the Southern Railway's main works at Eastleigh, a couple of the workmen standing alongside the track recognised the train for what it was and hurled stones from the track ballast at the carriages. Eastleigh had been the target of a heavy raid some months earlier. One stone broke a window in the front coach and several more damaged the paintwork on other coaches. Joe leaned out of the cab and yelled, "Bugger off, you lot!" Then a British guard opened a window and looked out; he aimed his rifle at the throwing workers, who ran; the guard laughed and shut the window again.

As they passed through Winchester, a small number of passengers on the platform noticed the German uniforms and booed loudly as the train passed.

"Did you hear that, Les?" said Joe to the driver.

"Hear what?"

"That booing from some passengers on the platform as we passed."

"No." Les was concentrating on his driving.

"At least," continued Joe, "they didn't throw anything."

"They were probably caught by surprise and didn't have anything to hand to throw," commented Les. "Some of them probably remember that raid on Eastleigh recently."

At Basingstoke, they turned off the Southern main line on to the Great Western track towards Reading, where they were directed into a carriage siding away from the platforms. They noticed some army catering staff, with tea urns on the platform for the army guards and POWs.

"I didn't think the Germans liked tea," remarked Les as Joe climbed down to uncouple their engine.

"They're going to have to get used to it; they'll be drinking it for a few years," replied Joe as he dropped to the ballast. He released the vacuum brake pipe and then strolled to the GWR crew at the other end of the train.

A Great Western Hall class 4-6-0 backed on to the train at the other end and its fireman, Tommy Hawkins, coupling his engine to the train, saw the approaching Southern fireman and waited for him. "Morning! Any problems so far?"

"Some workers at Eastleigh took exception to the POWs and chucked some stones at us, and passengers waiting at Winchester booed us we went by, but nothing really dramatic."

"Yeah, we've been cleared to run non-stop through all stations in case any locals get a bit ratty at seeing the Jerries, but we should be fine as only Brum and 'Hampton have had any bad raids. We'll have to be careful there."

"Well, good luck with them, then."

"Yes, ta. Cheerio." Tommy climbed back to his mate in the Hall.

"What did that Southern bloke tell you?" asked Driver Reg Smithers as Tommy stepped back into the cab.

"He said that they had no real problems, apart from a couple of workers in Eastleigh who chucked stones at them."

"Let's hope that's the worst that we get, an' all," muttered Reg.

They hurried through Didcot, Oxford, Banbury, Leamington Spa, Warwick on past Moor Street Station in Birmingham, and into the long tunnel before Snow Hill. But at Snow Hill they were signalled into the main down platform to stop.

"What the hell?" cried Reg angrily. "What bloody idiot directed us to stop here? We should have been sent through on the down relief so we could go through without stopping!"

The platform was crowded with passengers waiting for a down express to Birkenhead. They very soon noticed the train's passengers and an irate murmur began in the crowd. Some of the train's doors were being pulled open as angry civilians tried to climb aboard and give vent to their feelings about having enemy soldiers in their city. Inside the train, army guards were trying to wrestle out those who were trying to get in and to close the doors with only partial success. Other passengers were banging their fists on the sides of the coaches in their frustration and anger.

Two furious middle-aged ladies came up to the cab, one of them banging with her umbrellas on the cab side and demanding to know what the crew were doing.

Reg leaned out. "We're doing our job, madam," he said. "Why?"

"You've got a lot of Germans in your train!"

"Yes, we have. We're taking them to a prison camp."

"They should be shot for what they've done."

Reg blinked in astonishment. "You want us to shoot our prisoners?"

"Of course!"

"If we shoot our prisoners, the Germans will shoot theirs, so a lot of British soldiers would get killed!" Reg's anger mounted and he lost his temper. "Can't you see that, you daft old biddy!"

While the engine crew were having their altercation with the two ladies, one frightened prisoner had managed to avoid the army guard, who was busy at the platform door, and had climbed out of a door window on the other side of the train, dropping onto the track, where the people on the platform could not see him. In his panic, he ran across to the opposite empty up platform but did not see the approaching up freight train trundling sluggishly on the up through line. The engine's buffer beam hit him and knocked him back into the 'six foot way': the gap between two tracks. Tommy saw this and scrambled down to see if the German was badly injured. He ran over to the man, grabbed his arm and pulled him up. "Come on, mate," he shouted, "you'll get yourself killed if you're not careful." Tommy dragged the dazed man to the engine and heaved him up the steps and into the cab.

By this time, a number of troops with police had got the platform crowd under some form of control. All the doors were checked and inside the train the guards were checking the POW numbers. Reg leaned out and called a soldier over. "Climb up here, mate, we've got one of your blokes in the cab. He's been hurt."

The astounded soldier got into the cab and saw the POW. "What the 'ell's the bugger doin' 'ere?"

"We think he panicked and got out of a window, ran across the track and got hit by a passing freight. We can't get him back into the train without putting him on the platform. He'd get lynched by this angry mob."

"Aye, 'e would too," said the soldier feelingly, "I nearly got belted meself, when I tried to stop 'em gettin' at 'em in the train."

"We've got the green, Reg," said Tommy, looking back down the platform at the train guard's flag. The driver eased the regulator up and the train moved off, with the angry crowd still yelling abuse. But 200 yards further on, Reg eased the train to a stop once more so that they could transfer the errant POW and the soldier back into the train. Once this was done, they moved off again.

"You wouldn't credit it, Tommy," commented Reg as

they accelerated away from Birmingham. "Two months back, I was in the Old Oak Common shelter during an air raid and cursing the bastards. Now here we are, saving the sods from being murdered by some of our own bloody people!"

14 - A breath of fresh air (October 1943)

The savage and frightening days of the Blitz were mostly over, yet in spite of the increasing RAF strength over Britain and the anti-aircraft batteries, Manchester, like other big cities in the United Kingdom, still suffered raids from the Luftwaffe. A recent attack had targeted arms factories and railway yards. Enemy bombers had probably intended to attack the docks along the Manchester Ship Canal, and the Royal Ordnance Factory at Patricroft, but housing areas of Salford also received attention from a flight of bombers, and the residents had suffered accordingly.

Driver Dick Veno and Fireman Jim Carter had brought in the Manchester businessmen's Club Train from Llandudno into Manchester's Exchange station that morning and were due to return to their home shed at Chester 'on the cushions'; the term for enginemen travelling in comfort in a coach. They were waiting on a station bench for the Manchester to Rhyl local, due to leave as soon as the platform at which they had brought their train in had been cleared and the local brought in. On the Manchester approaches past Patricroft, Eccles and Salford, they had been saddened at the bombsites on both sides of the tracks, many houses of which were supported by massive beams, to prevent them from falling on to passing pedestrians before they could be demolished and later rebuilt.

While they waited, Dick bought a *Manchester Guardian* newspaper to peruse on the returning train. His mate had pulled a much-thumbed Hank Jansen novel out of his pocket. Dick knew this was pornographic and almost certainly illegal. With the folded paper on his lap, he spent a few moments observing his surroundings

Like all Manchester's stations, Exchange was in its normal wartime state, with filthy locomotives and grubby rolling stock after years of poor maintenance, some hastily repaired trackwork, and new brickwork to replace parts of the damaged buildings; not to mention the barrage balloons in the sky to deter attacking enemy aircraft. The general dreariness was in stark contrast to the sunlight of a late October morning.

A large and grimy 2-6-4T tank engine had just arrived from Runcorn with a rake of non-corridor coaches filled with morning shoppers. Most carried small lunch packets, consisting of sandwiches spread sparingly with margarine and jam, a smear of Marmite, or even lettuce leaves, while luckier ones had thin slices of Spam, saved by careful husbanding of coupons from their ration books and a friendly grocer. A York to Liverpool express hauled by another grimy dark red locomotive; this time a Jubilee class 4-6-0, slowed down as it approached the station, heading along the immensely long joint through platform linking Manchester's Victoria station with Exchange. At something like half a mile in length, this platform was claimed to be the longest in Britain. The long train, with its LMS maroon coaches and a couple of LNER teak coaches, on a through service from Newcastle, passed slowly along the Victoria platform before coming to a stop in Exchange for a brief pause. The whole scene, mused Dick Veno, had become like life itself in wartime; drab, depressing, and rather boring.

As he sat he wondered how long the war was going to last. The BBC announcer on the wireless the previous evening seemed to suggest that the tide of war was gradually turning in favour of the Allies, now that the Americans were sending their troops over to Britain in large numbers. Rommel had been stopped in El Alamein and chased out of North Africa. The Allies were now pushing the Germans north through Italy.

But although there were signs of optimism, for Britons the end could not come soon enough; they were very tired of the Blackout, the rationing of so many basic products in both food and clothing, of standing in crowded trains for hours on end, of being restricted to having a bath in a mere seven inches of water, and of watery ice cream.

Enterprising children, however, who had hardly known the luxury of what had been available in peacetime, were occasionally seen tackling American servicemen with the cry of 'Got any gum, Chum?' This often brought them a smile and a couple of sweets or a stick of chewing gum from soldiers, who all seemed to have a soft spot for British children.

Thinking of children put Dick's mind to his own young son. He had bought their six-year-old a clockwork Hornby train just before the war and delighted in playing with it with the boy. The cheerful red 4-4-2 engine was named *Royal Scot*, although apart from the nameplate it bore it had no resemblance whatever to the big LMS 4-6-0 of that name. (The tooling had been designed by French Hornby, and similar engines had been supplied as *Lord Nelson*, *Caerphilly Castle* and *Flying Scotsman,* all requiring equal fantasy to be seen as those famous locomotives.) Nevertheless, the pleasure it gave to both of them had been well worth the price paid, and it certainly looked a good deal cleaner than any of the LMS engines James Carter had seen for many months. It was now a long time since he had seen a Hornby train in a toyshop, he realised with regret. He would have liked to acquire a few more wagons or coaches for their railway, but Meccano Ltd had turned of course to manufacturing precision components for military equipment, and toy trains and Dinky toys were no longer available except, rarely, in second-hand shops.

Dick's mind turned to the future. "What do you think, Jim," he asked his mate, "about what these bombed areas like Salford will look like after twenty years?"

"Eh? What?" Jim Carter's mind was still rooted (if that is the right word) in his novel with Private Investigator Randy Lawless, watching through a window the vigorous rhythmic gymnastics of a wayward husband in bed with his shapely secretary. "What's that?"

"Get what passes for your mind off that trash, Jim. I asked what you think Salford will look like in twenty years' time, after it's all been rebuilt?"

"How the hell do I know, Dick? What's it matter, anyway?

You and I won't be there. Listen," he said holding up his book, "this bloke in bed with his bird has had her at least three—"

At that moment their conversation was interrupted by the sight of another train, arriving from the direction of Victoria.

"Good God almighty!" breathed Driver Veno. "Look at that!" He could hardly believe his eyes. The approaching train was incredible. It was double-headed, with a gleaming, polished and spotless Black Five 4-6-0 locomotive. The engine, clearly a pilot, was followed by a Jubilee class 4-6-0 train engine in similar condition, hauling a short rake of equally immaculate coaches.

"Cripes!" Fireman Carter was similarly startled. "What the hell?"

Neither man had seen anything like this in five years, and even back then no train had been as immaculate as this one was; even the locomotive buffers were polished steel. The two men hadn't paid much attention to the group of smartly-dressed officials on the platform opposite where the new train was pulling in but as the train drew gently to a stand most of the officials moved to the door of one of the central coaches. The door opened and an attendant stood back to make room for a slight man in the uniform of an RAF Air Marshall, who descended from the coach to be greeted by a number of dignitaries.

"It's the King!" exclaimed Dick, recognising the man who had often appeared in the newsreels, visiting bombed areas with the Queen. "And that must be the Royal Train!" Both men knew that the LMS had built a specially armoured set of coaches for the Royal Train in 1941, at the height of the Blitz, but neither had seen them before. His Majesty King George VI looked around and shook hands with a couple of the party, who were waiting to greet him, and was then escorted from the platform. After about fifteen minutes the Royal Train moved off slowly and Dick Veno wondered where it would be stabled overnight. The locomotives, he knew, would need to be checked and serviced, probably at Patricroft, and the coaches would be taken to a place of safety, but he couldn't think of anywhere local between

Manchester and Liverpool that would be completely safe from attack; Newton-le-Willows had a large railway factory and even near Warrington, further south the Americans had an air base at Padgate; both potential Luftwaffe targets.

After the formalities were over, the Royal Train moved out, again heading west.

In the meantime, their own local to Rhyl had arrived in the bay. They chose an empty compartment and settled down to their reading; Driver Veno to his newspaper and Fireman Carter enthralled in the adventures (and detailed observations) of PI Lawless. They had a half-hour wait until their train was due to depart for the North Wales coast. As they passed Patricroft, they noticed on their left the two Royal Train engines being serviced.

"Wonder where the coaches are?" queried Dick Veno, but there was no response from his fireman, who was trying to re-order the loose and well-thumbed pages of his grubby paperback. Dick sighed and shook his head as he returned to his *Manchester Guardian*.

However, as they passed the Mickle Trafford junction with the LNER route into Chester, they saw the Royal Train coaches being hauled by a remarkably clean D11 Director class 4-4-0, heading south west on the Cheshire Lines route.

"So that's where they're stabling the train, Jim," said Dick to his mate. "They're putting it into Northgate station. They must be planning to bring the King by car to Chester tomorrow to pick up his train."

"In Chester?" said Jim, looking up, startled. This was an error because his book slipped out of his hands and fell in a jumbled heap of loose pages on the floor. "Bugger!" he said vehemently, "now I won't be able to finish the damn book before we get 'ome, and if my missus sees it, she'll-" he paused. "Listen Dick, could you do me a favour and-"

"No fear, mate," his driver replied quickly. "What d'you think Anne would say if she caught me with that nonsense? Give it to Henry at the shed. He likes that sort of literature."

"If he gets it, I'll never see it again!" moaned Jim.

Next morning, as Driver Veno and Fireman Carter booked on duty at Chester's LMS shed, they saw immediately that the two Royal Train engines had steamed from Patricroft and were getting a last-minute check-up from shed staff and cleaners. Today, the two enginemen were booked on a North Wales passenger service to Bangor, with a 4-4-0 Compound engine. Dick Veno liked these engines; they were ideal for fast passenger services with a modest load. As they backed on to their train on Platform 4, they noticed the royal coaches being pushed into Platform 10, opposite a big Stanier 2-6-4T tank engine, this time clean but not by no means immaculate. Once it had eased the coaches gently up to the two Royal Train engines waiting at the end of the platform, it reversed, leaving the train ready move out towards Crewe and, presumably, London Euston.

"Wonder where the King spent the night?" mused Driver Veno.

"'E spent it at 'The Blossoms'," remarked Jim Carter. "That posh hotel in Eastgate Street."

Dick Veno stared at his mate, "How do you know that? I didn't realise you moved in such refined circles. Fancy you having the necessary to be able to afford staying at 'The Blossoms'! Did you perchance have breakfast with the King, Sir James?"

"Nah! I was on the Chester Corporation bus an' saw the Daimler and a few other flash cars parked outside the 'otel on me way to work."

"Well, that's a relief; at least he was spared from your offer to let him read that grubby book of yours!"

15 - No Immunity for visitors (November 1943)

The small group of American Army Air Force men in their green uniforms were strolling down Regent Street, looking at the shops and bewildered at the paucity of goods on display. One of them asked a passer-by why there was so little in the shops.

The elderly man, walking with the aid of a stick, looked surprised at the question. "Why sir, we're at war, and goods from overseas are hard to come by. The U-boats are taking a heavy toll on our ships."

"Yeah, but now we GIs are here to support you Limeys things should be better."

"We are, of course, very grateful for American support, but remember that we've been at war for over four years now and apart from our Empire we've been pretty much on our own for more than half that time."

"Mmm – yeah, I guess so."

The Americans walked on until a cry of surprise came from the burly corporal among them; "Hey, you guys, lookit that!" What caught the attention of Corporal Hiram J Henderson of the United States Army Air Force, just ahead of them, was a trio of RAF airmen, one of whom was black. Corporal Henderson hurried up to the RAF men and addressed a Leading Aircraftman.

"Hey bud, why're you with this nigger? What's he done?"

The RAF man glared at the American. "Done, Corporal? He's done nothing; he's our flight sergeant."

"Your flight sergeant? But he's black!" Corporal Henderson's shocked gaze rested on the sergeant's sleeves, with their three chevrons and a crown. Flight Sergeant Bill Stimson interposed coldly, "Is there something we can do for you, Corporal?"

Henderson glared at the Flight Sergeant. "You talkin' to me, boy?"

Flight Sergeant Stimson snapped, "I am not your boy! You'll address me as 'Flight Sergeant'. Even in your air force, I outrank you."

"But – but, you're – er, black!"

"Ah! You noticed?"

"But blackies don't get to senior ranks in our air force."

"You may also have noticed that I'm not in your air force; I'm in the RAF, where we do things differently."

"Okay, no offence."

"No offence, *Flight Sergeant*!"

"Sure, sure; no offence, Flight Sergeant."

With that, Bill Stimson and the RAF men stalked on, leaving the surprised Americans wondering what other surprises were in store for them in this 'tight little island'.

It wasn't too long before they found another. Advised that a train from Waterloo Station would get them to their base, on the platform at Waterloo they stared at the ancient and diminutive tank engine, which brought their coaches in, and a porter told them they had a twenty-minute wait before the train would leave. Two of the airmen were breathing in the steam and smoke with obvious interest and familiarity, and on hearing of the wait they told Corporal Henderson that they were railwaymen themselves and they wanted to have a chat with the driver.

"See if he's a nigger, too," were Henderson's parting words.

The two airmen walked to the front of their train, where a Lord Nelson class 4-6-0 had backed on. The fireman had coupled the engine to the train and was climbing back onto the platform when he saw the Americans examining the engine with a professional interest.

"You blokes interested in trains?"

One of them nodded. "I was an engineer with the New York Central until Uncle Sam called; and my friend here was a stoker with the Pennsy. You guys have cute little trains here." He grinned and added, "Are you sure this little engine can pull this here train?"

Fireman 'Sandy' Willis laughed. "Little engine?" he said. "This is one of our biggest passenger engines! But come up into the cab and meet my driver." The two Americans nodded their thanks and clambered with alacrity into the cab, where introductions all round were made.

"You're an engineer?" queried Driver Forbes.

"Yeah, but I guess you would say 'driver'," replied Al Seddons, "and what you call a fireman we call a 'stoker'. But I have to say your engines are very different from ours. They're much smaller, and," as he looked out along the firebox and boiler, "somehow much cleaner looking."

"Yes," replied Driver Forbes, "I've seen pictures of American locomotives – they certainly are huge, and seem to have everything hanging on outside the boiler, whereas we put most of our bits underneath and out of sight."

"How heavy is this train?" asked the American stoker curiously.

"We've about 450 tons on today."

"450 tons? And this engine can handle that weight?"

"Easily; she was built to handle over 500 on the flat, at over sixty miles an hour."

"Geez, I'd never have thought that! Could she—"

"Geoff, we've got five minutes," interrupted Fireman Sandy Willis.

"Sorry lads," said the driver, "I'll have to ask you to leave the cab, we're off soon and we still—"

"Yeah of course," replied the American hurriedly, "thanks for the look around, we'll be back on leave in a week or two and we might see you again."

"We're on this run for another month, so you'd be welcome if you come early."

"We will." And the Americans made their way back to their compartment, chatting about the English trains. Al, the ex-engineer, told his mate that he was determined to see the two English crewmen again, to find out more about how the 'little English' engines worked. He wanted to see if he could get some leave and check it out.

"I'll come too," said ex-stoker Bert Freeman, "I liked those two guys."

Neither of the men could have had any idea of the consequences which were to follow their intention.

It was a fortnight before the two Americans had leave, and they made their way to Waterloo, where they hoped to see Driver Forbes and Fireman Willis once more. They were in luck; the two crewmen still had the same shift and were delighted to see the two airmen again, inviting them into the cab a second time, this time of a King Arthur class 4-6-0.

"We've only got 345 tons on this train, so we don't need a big engine today," explained Geoff. "But look, fellas, if you're here when we return at about 7.45 tonight, we'll take you both to the shed at Nine Elms and you can see how one of our sheds works. Our train arrives on Platform 7."

"Gee, thanks Geoff," Al was delighted at the thought. "We'll be here on the dot, won't we Bert?"

Bert's face mirrored Alf's enthusiasm. "Platform 7? For sure!"

The two airmen spent part of the afternoon wandering around Waterloo and were waiting eagerly on Platform 7 when a heavy train pulled in at 7.45pm, drawn by one of the most remarkable looking engines they had ever seen.

"What in tarnation is that?" Bert gasped; this engine was bigger than anything they had seen that day and looked more like a coach without windows than a locomotive. It had smooth, slab-like sides, which matched those of the coaches in its train. It drew to a stop and then they saw Sandy Willis climb out of the cab to uncouple the engine, ready for the shunting tank to draw the coaches away to the sidings.

They were standing next to Sandy as he climbed back up onto the platform and he recognised them, flashing a welcoming smile.

"Hi, Yanks!" he grinned. "Come on up into the cab, Geoff will be pleased to see you again."

They found themselves in the cab of this great Merchant Navy class 4-6-2. Driver Forbes greeted them but told them to stay put as he got the signal to back out of the station.

"I was hoping we might see you two again," he said with one hand on the regulator as they backed down the platform. "If you've got time, you could come into the shed with us; the Shedmaster has given his permission."

The two Americans nodded their gratitude. "That'd be great, and we don't have to be back in camp until tomorrow night," replied Bert.

The four men climbed down from the cab once they reached the big shed at Nine Elms and handed the locomotive over to the shed staff for servicing. The Americans were shown the ash disposal pits, the coaling facilities and turntable, and then they were taken into the enginemen's mess. Here, they were introduced to the strong Southern Railway tea and they sampled one man's sandwiches of 'bread and dripping' (which they did not at all fancy). They were appalled at the elementary facilities available to these British crewmen, thinking of their own far more luxurious comforts in the USA.

"D'ya reckon I could have another look in one of your cabs?" asked Bert. "They are so different from ours."

"Of course," said Sandy. "I'll take you into one while Al and Geoff are finishing their tea. Then we'll meet again back here."

Sandy took Bert over to a nearby King Arthur locomotive, which was having a minor repair. The fitter was fastening the retaining bolts on one of the coupling rods and smiled as they mounted the steps into the cab. "Don't take your mate for a ride, Sandy; I haven't finished tightening this rod!"

"I'm only a fireman, Amos," responded Sandy with a grin, "Taking this 'Arthur' for a ride would be very naughty!" Once in the cab, he began to explain what the duties of an English fireman were.

But while they were discussing the differences between English and American firing practices, the air raid sirens began to sound their urgent warning wails.

"Ah, fuck it!" snarled Sandy. "Those aircraft engines sound too close and we're too far away from the shelter. Quick, Bert, this firebox is cold, we can climb in and it'll be a bit cramped but we'll get good protection from any flying shrapnel!" Bert wriggled in first, followed by Sandy, who pulled the fire door to. They both sat in the firebox and leaned against the inside wall of the backhead. Sandy pulled out his fags and offered one to his friend and they smoked quietly while the bombs began to fall outside.

Driver Geoff Forbes, still in the mess with his guest, took Al quickly to the shelter, where they sat with other crewmen, listening to the falling bombs. These were so close that it was clear that the railway complex was the target for the evening.

In the King Arthur firebox, Bert heard the thumps of falling bombs and cracks of shards of metal hitting the sides of their locomotive. He was heartily thankful they were safe inside this most unusual refuge.

"Don't worry too much, Bert," said Sandy. "We've got a layer of steel and two layers of copper between us and the raid outside. We're pretty safe against anything but a direct hit." In this, he was accurate; it was by no means unknown for shedmen, finding themselves near an unlit and dormant locomotive during an air raid, to climb into the firebox for safety.

Driver Forbes, in the shedmen's shelter, spent the time of the raid outlining to Al some of the hazards of railway life under the bombing; this gave the American railwayman a different – and very personal – appreciation of what British railway crews went through. The raid continued for another half-hour before it ended with one final explosion, so close it shook the whole shelter.

"Christ, that was close!" grunted Geoff as the sirens began the steady 'All Clear!' tone, signifying that it was safe to come out of the shelters again.

"Hey, what about Bert and Sandy?" asked Al anxiously.

"Hmm," Geoff frowned. "They were in the shed. I expect Sandy will have taken Bert into a cold firebox somewhere; they shouldn't have come to too much harm."

"Into a *firebox*?" Al couldn't believe his ears.

"Can you think of a safer place in an emergency?"

"Well, now you mention it – er, no."

The crews leaving the shelter were met with a scene of devastation; there were bomb craters on many of the tracks and damaged locomotives, overturned vans and wagons could be seen among the twisted and broken rails. The shed itself seemed unharmed, except for a large hole in the roof, where a bomb had fallen and scored a direct hit on a locomotive. It was clear that this shattered engine was totally destroyed, as were the two railwaymen who had been sheltering inside its firebox.

16 - The female of the species (February 1944)

The war had been going on for four and a half years by now but in some ways the scene at Eastbourne Station was, apart from a certain shabbiness, scarcely different from its pre-war prim and proper appearance, until one looked closer. The platform chocolate- and cigarette-machines had long been empty and the platform edges were painted white so that they could be distinguished in the Blackout; inside the station cafeteria, the goods on display were only basic in range. Tea and buns could be bought but the wide variety of snacks of pre-war days was gone. A peacetime observer might be surprised at the proportion of military uniforms among the waiting passengers and he or she might have noticed that the ticket collector at the gate, and two of the porters were female.

Indeed, the number of women in railway service was causing problems in the Lancing coach maintenance works. Mr Warren, the union rep, was arguing fiercely with a young woman, Elsie Dickson, in the office of the manager, Mr Manning. Bert Warren wanted no more females to be employed as they were taking jobs from the men and he was concerned that the men away at war would not get their jobs back. Elsie, on the other hand, was adamant that the females were perfectly competent at their jobs. The constant bickering was affecting the efficiency of the works. Mr Manning could see both sides of the situation and was left wondering what he could do to solve his dilemma and speed up the maintenance of the works.

The First Class compartment of the early-morning Southern Electric express to London Bridge was full. Four of the six City gentlemen had their noses buried in their copies of the *Times* but the remaining two were engaged in conversation, if conversation was an appropriate word, as the younger one was given little opportunity to advance his own views on the matter under discussion.

"Mark my words, Callington, I have every respect for what our brave lads are doing to the Hun in Italy but why in heaven's name does our government here at home allow our womenfolk out of their kitchens to do work which only men are capable of?"

Edward Penberthy was a tall, dignified business executive, his bowler and briefcase neatly placed on the luggage rack above. His *Times* lay on his knee, where he could easily lift it and hide behind it, thus avoiding having to listen to someone else's contribution.

"It's my understanding, Mr Penberthy, that the jobs are only until the men return from—"

"D'you know," continued Penberthy, paying no attention at all to what his younger colleague was trying to say, "I watched a female shunter last week walking along the tracks at Hailsham. She had a shunter's pole over her shoulder and was walking along as if she knew what to do with it. Now I ask you, how can a woman lift the heavy chains of a coupling between wagons? And what will she do when the sudden hiss of a vacuum pipe goes off? She'll jump six feet into the air!"

"Well, sir, it's my view that—"

"You know what the problem is, Callington?" continued Penberthy. "It's that senior railway officials will not stand up to these women. They are just unable to see that what the women want is quite out of the question. There are jobs and duties on the railway which females simply cannot manage, due to their weaker physique and emotional limitations. I will admit, however, that there are possibly – I say only possibly – one or two jobs which a female might in an emergency be capable of. Ticket-checking at the station entrances, they appear to be able to manage, but did you see those female porters actually *carrying* a suitcase? Seriously, anything else would be a disaster for the railway companies."

At this moment, the compartment door slid open and a ticket collector came in. The two men looked up in surprise to see a young lady in a railway uniform, a ticket punch in her hand.

"Tickets please, gentlemen," she said with a disarming smile. "And I am sorry to tell you that this train has been redirected to Victoria and we will be arriving in London twenty minutes later than stated in the timetable." She began to peruse and punch their tickets.

"One moment, young lady." Penberthy's indignant voice overruled other murmurs of disappointment in the compartment. "I have an important business meeting in the City, with the military authorities, for which I have to be on time!"

The guard smiled at him. "Yes, I'm sure you have, sir; and I expect all these other gentlemen have important business meetings at which they too must be present. Regrettably, there is nothing I can do about the diversion."

"Then I shall have to inform the Southern Railway management of my, er – and the army's – serious displeasure."

"Of course, sir, you have every right to do that; however, the problem is not of the Southern Railway's making. The army has requisitioned platforms at London Bridge for supplies for two troop trains, and their requirements override those of the railway company. I suggest, therefore, that you direct your complaint to the military authorities." She addressed her final remarks to the whole compartment: "Once more, gentlemen, I regret the inconvenience and wish you all a very good morning." She withdrew and slid the door shut.

Penberthy's face was red with anger and embarrassment. "Can you believe the impertinence of the woman?" he demanded of his colleague, and continued without allowing any reply to his question, "It just goes to prove that these women are getting above themselves!" In his anger he failed to notice that his ticket did not slip into his waistcoat pocket as intended but fell to the floor.

Edward Penberthy's frustration with female railway workers was to continue. As they paused at Norwood

Junction, they observed a waiting passenger train on an adjacent platform. A female wheeltapper was slowly working along the train, tapping the wheels and listening carefully to the ringing sound. She paused at one wheel, tapped it again, listened and shook her head. She strode off to find the guard, returning with him and pointing to the wheel. She tapped it again and explained something to him. The locomotive fireman was directed to uncouple the coach, which was then drawn off. By this time, their own train was on the move again but before Penberthy could explode, one of the other men at the window turned his neighbour and said, "Isn't that interesting! That wheeltapper has found a faulty wheel and has possibly saved that train full of passengers from a serious accident." He addressed the others in the compartment and added, "My nephew's a wheeltapper. He taps each wheel and listens. If it rings true, he goes to the next, but if it sounds like a cracked plate he knows the metal has a hairline crack, which could lead to the entire wheel fracturing, derailing the carriage, and possibly the whole train. If this happened in the path of an oncoming train, the death toll could be considerable."

Penberthy remained silent; he was quite prepared to browbeat his young colleague, but tackling a man who seemed to know his subject was rather a different matter. He hid his red face behind his *Times* and maintained a lofty disregard for his fellow travellers.

The train trundled over the Thames and down the Grosvenor bank into Victoria, slowing as it entered the station throat, clattering over the points and pulling into the platform. Most passengers hurried out to the exits to the street, or to the Underground to catch buses, trams or tube trains to their final destinations. Callington noticed that his older colleague took his time collecting his bowler and briefcase from the rack, carefully folding his newspaper before leaving the train and walking in a relaxed manner to the open barrier.

"Will you not be late for your urgent meeting with the

army this morning, Mr Penberthy?" he asked as he passed his colleague.

"Meeting?" queried the latter. "Why on earth do you think I've got a meeting, Callington?"

"Oh, er—" Callington muttered in confusion, "I'm sorry, I understood you to tell the ticket collector that—"

"Oh, that woman. No, I don't have any meeting; not today at any rate," he added. "But you can't let women have the last word."

As they strolled past the front of the train he noticed the motorman chatting sociably with the lady guard. "Hrmph!" he muttered quietly to Callington in annoyance. "That driver's weakened already; the country's going to the dogs!"

Callington's grunt was non-committal; he knew that his colleague was on the defensive. As far as he was concerned, as long as railway staff were competent, it didn't really matter whether they were male or female, but he knew that Penberthy's goodwill might be important for his own future career prospects.

Callington showed his ticket to the female ticket inspector at the barrier and passed through the gate but he heard her stop Penberthy, saying, "Have you a valid ticket, sir?"

Penberthy stopped, searching his pocket for his ticket. "Er – I seem to have misplaced it. I will have to purchase another one."

"I'm afraid that's not good enough, sir, you will need to..."

"Young lady," interrupted Penberthy angrily, "I travel on this train every day, and have done so for eleven years without any difficulties before. I will give you my name and address and tomorrow I will show you a valid weekly ticket."

"That will not do, sir," she replied. "You have travelled today without a valid ticket, and that is an offence and must be reported."

"Now, let's not be hasty," said Penberthy in a sudden conciliatory tone. He pulled out a ten-shilling note from his wallet. "I know you ladies are often a little short of cash, so what if you were to...?"

"I think you should put that note away, sir," she replied coldly. "Your name and address, please? For my report," she added, taking a notebook and pencil from her pocket.

"Report? Nonsense!" By now Penberthy was furious but before he could pour more oil on the fire, a nearby railway policeman walked over and said to the ticket collector, "Is there a problem here, Miss?"

"Yes, Officer," answered the inspector. "This man has travelled without a ticket and has tried to bribe me to forget the matter."

"I see," said the Constable and he grasped Penberthy's arm firmly. "You are under arrest, sir. That money would have been better spent in paying your fare. The police office is not far." And Penberthy was marched off.

Back in Lancing, the works manager had come to a conclusion which he hoped would bring the warring parties together. He called them both into his office.

"I've asked you both to come and try to settle your differences," he said as they sat down. "Quite frankly, I have had enough and want a better and more efficient work programme."

"It's all these women you're employing, Mr Manning," said Bert. "They can't do their jobs properly."

"That's bloody nonsense, Bert Warren!" Elsie Dickson was angry. "Our girls are well trained and they know their stuff; you know that as well as I do."

"*Our* girls, Elsie?' demanded Bert. "Since when 'ave you bin a union rep?"

Manning could see this developing into another all-out brawl in his office, which wasn't going to help. He lifted his hand to stop further argument. "Miss Dickson," he began, "not only will your girls have their jobs guaranteed until the men return, I will continue to appoint new girls to the work as long as they can demonstrate competence."

"And Mr Warren," he continued, "Any man who worked for us before being called up will get his job back. That is definite, and," he paused, seeing Elsie's eyes glinting in anger, "there will be no further discussion on this point."

Bert sat back in his chair and eyed Elsie with a triumphant grin. Manning caught sight of this. "Oh," he added. "One further detail; I want an efficient workplace, and any future argument about who does which job will result in the instant dismissal of whoever complains. Male or female."

That, he thought, should put an end to the constant arguments between Elsie and Bert. But he was quite wrong there. Not six months later, Bert Warren and Elsie Dickson were married.

17 - The ammunition train (March 1944)

The Great Western Railway's 28xx class 2-8-0 engine, one of Mr Churchward's first designs, originally appeared in 1902, and was intended for heavy freight work throughout the GWR system. In this, the engine was superlative, and Driver Ernie Tipson and his fireman Harry Earnshaw, of Bristol's St Philip Marsh shed, were happy that this, their rostered engine, was still soldiering on almost thirty years later. The 28xxs had been well built and were popular with their crews, due to their general reliability. Nevertheless, rolling stock at this juncture during the war was not always getting the regular maintenance necessary to maintain pre-war standards. Many of the men who would normally be employed in this work were now in the armed forces, and their peacetime work was sometimes done by women under training. Senior employers were frequently surprised by the competence shown by the new female labour force, although the young women lacked the long experience of the pre-war male employees. Female shunters and even porters were frequently seen among the myriad duties previously thought to be all-male responsibilities.

Ernie backed the engine slowly and very cautiously onto its train. The reason for this unusual procedure lay in the heavily loaded twenty-four vehicles full of explosives. There were, of course, no fuses in the RAF bombs, yet railway personnel always treated such military loads with particular care; they could too readily visualise what would happen if the whole lot blew up, and were inclined to handle the shunting procedures very gingerly.

Near Corsham in Wiltshire, the secret underground ammunition storage base had a rail connection to the GWR main line to the west, and this particular freight was due to leave at 5.30pm, bound for a bomber base in Lincolnshire. On arrival there, the load would be handed over to the RAF to be ready for softening up the German support units once the Normandy landings, which even the Germans were expecting in the not-too-distant future, had taken place. There were already top-secret camps and storage areas in East Anglia, and frequent freight trains could be seen heading that way. What very few people knew, however, was that within these eastern storage areas the lines of tanks and heavy trucks were made largely of plywood and were intended to falsely suggest a planned landing across the North Sea; the genuine effort was concentrated on the South Coast ports.

A further reason for the crewmen's concern was that while the Germans had been driven out of North Africa, they hadn't yet lost all of their air force and German fighter aircraft still made occasional 'hit and run' raids across the country, trains being a common target.

Driver 'Tipsy' (to his mates) glanced at his fireman. "Make sure you keep yer eyes peeled, Harry," he growled. "The bloody Luftwaffe might 'ave a fighter with our monikers on it." Harry nodded and kept on shovelling, to ensure that Tipsy was able to keep their freight engine moving at a steady pace east via Devizes, Newbury and Didcot, to Banbury. Here, they were to hand over the freight to an LNER crew and their locomotive for further transport to the bomber base. The enginemen began to breathe more easily as the sky gradually grew dark, making spotting them much more difficult; although the tarpaulin cover over the cab and tender front could not entirely hide the light from the fire hole from prying Teutonic eyes. If a lucky enemy pilot spotted them, he could make himself into a very serious nuisance. Such attacks as these were becoming rare now that Fighter Command was proving itself well able to deal the few daring German pilots who got over the Channel; nevertheless, the occasional fighter still made it through, even if it didn't always get back to base, and an attack on a munitions train could make a tidy bang.

Driver Tipson and Fireman Earnshaw had taken munitions trains before and were always aware of what could happen, and very glad whenever they reached their destination safely and could leave their hazardous cargo to another crew. On this occasion, they were detoured over a lesser-used route, so as not to obstruct more urgent traffic, and, it has to be admitted, to reduce the chance of a major 'event', as the euphemism had it, which might even close the main line if anything untoward were to occur. Both men kept a sharp lookout for any smoke issuing from the vans' axleboxes, along the string of vehicles, or for any signalman's frantic gestures.

A hot box was when the oil leaked out of an axlebox; the metal-upon-metal friction would generate red heat, igniting any residual oil or grease and then, if not quickly attended to, it could set fire to the van and even the whole train. Railwaymen did not like such events in their vicinity and normally took all reasonable precautions. But, as Robert Burns once wrote: *"The best laid schemes o' Mice an' Men, gang aft agley."*

It was not simply the rolling stock where maintenance was not now up to the required safety standards; the track itself did not always get the attention such an important part of the system needed. Admittedly, trackwork repair after a bombing raid had been brought to a fine art, and while the general public was scarcely aware of it, absolute wonders of replacement after bomb damage had become the norm on the busiest routes, in order to maintain the heavy wartime traffic demands on the railways.

Regrettably, this was not always the case where minor adjustments were needed, and this time it was to have tragic consequences. Constant heavy usage could loosen the chair blocks out of the chairs and fishplate bolts could work loose; both of which could alter the gauge or cause the rails to sink, and rails due for replacement could even actually break under the repeated pounding of heavy traffic.

Maisie Wetherspoon was a thoughtless girl but was both young and attractive, with an eye for any smart young man.

She was bewailing the lack of such commodities to her colleague on the clerical team in the Permanent Way office, where she had just taken a position as typist. It had been good fortune which had got her the job because her typing skill was mediocre at best. However, she was also very obliging and good-natured, and would have been horrified to know that she was about to set in motion a series of minor errors which were to have catastrophic results a hundred miles distant.

She was typing out a letter of instruction for the replacement of several older rails on an alternative main line with some from a nearby siding, but forgot to include the instruction that the ganger foreman should check them carefully before using them. Her boss glanced at the letter, sighing as he noticed the spelling mistakes, but he was too busy to have her retype them correctly; he didn't notice the sentence was missing, either.

Foreman Ganger Ben Trounson had retired in 1938 but had volunteered to return to his job as the war swallowed the men the GWR had counted on to fill the vacancies in railway work. He knew his job thoroughly but at the age of sixty-eight he was getting tired of the outdoor nature of his work. Furthermore, permanent way work needed strong young men who could lift. Sleepers and rails were very heavy, and it was hard to get enough suitable conscientious objectors to fill the gaps in the work gangs. The bitterly cold March weather over the Cotswolds was not helping, as they manhandled another rail to replace the one they had just removed from the single track route running line. Ben gave the replacement rail only a cursory glance and missed the hairline crack, the result of an earlier derailment, which was underneath the head. One of the new platelayers easing the rail into place and fastening the fishplate noticed the damage but assumed the foreman had seen and accepted it as safe, so made no comment.

During the night, several trains had hurried over the replaced rail, each putting a severe strain on it. At about 5.45am, when the weight of Tipsy's 28xx impacted it, it actually broke under the second van, snapping the coupling and parting the train. The train was vacuum fitted and so when the vacuum pipe stretched and broke, the vacuum brakes were automatically applied, slowing the whole train. As they were on a slight downward gradient, the rest of the train followed to a gradual stop and when the locomotive and van finally came to a halt, the rest of the train was only a few yards behind.

Ernie knew instantly that the train had parted but didn't know why. "Right, Harry," he said, "nip out and tell the guard what's happened an' he'll have to get a couple of detonators on the track be'ind us to warn any followin' train. I'll pull this van away to the next box an' warn the bobby."

Harry dropped down but before he could go to warn the guard he noticed in the dark a strong, acrid smell coming from the van's axlebox.

"Bloody hell!" he whispered, then shouted urgently to his driver, "Ernie!"

Ernie put his head out of the cab. "What?'

"We've got a hot box!"

"Oh Christ!" Ernie grabbed the coal watering pipe and tried to squirt a stream of cold water onto the axlebox but the wind blew most of it off course, with only a few drops hissing as they landed on the hot box.

"Get going, lad!" yelled Ernie, "An' I'll pull the van away from the rest of the train before the whole bloody lot goes up!"

Loosening the brake, he began to move downhill with the van. He stopped the train at the box and yelled out to the bobby to bring a bucket of water out. By this time, the hot box had caught light and set fire to the timbers of the wooden van body.

Ernie was too late. The fire in the axlebox had reached the floor of the van and five bombs went up in a colossal explosion.

In a sense, Driver Tipson was fortunate, as was the signalman in the adjacent box; neither of them knew anything about the explosion. They were killed instantly.

Very little of the signalbox itself, or the van, could be recognised in the daylight of the next morning. The locomotive was thrown onto its side forty yards away, and lay just outside the huge crater: twenty feet deep and thirty-five feet across. Windows in a nearby village had been shattered and eleven houses had been structurally damaged and had to be demolished. The locomotive was loaded on to a flatbed wagon and ferried to Swindon for a final examination, before being sent for scrapping.

Since much of the track had also been totally destroyed, there was no real evidence left as to what had caused the huge explosion, and the subsequent inquiry was left with an open verdict. There was nothing in the personal records of any of the four men killed which could reveal anything to account for any carelessness or incompetence. Driver Tipson and the signalman, as well as Fireman Earnshaw and the guard, all had impeccable records. All were very experienced railwaymen and well respected among their colleagues. Driver Ernie Tipson was awarded the George Cross posthumously and Fireman Earnshaw also received a medal for his bravery. The matter could not be kept out of the press, of course, but it was implied that faulty explosives were to blame.

One driver commented, "It were nice of them up there to hand out them medals, but let's face it; many of us is ferryin' explosives around the country, an' we all knows wot we 'ave ter do if there's a problem. They was only doin' wot they was trained to do."

Maisie Wetherspoon and her boss and Chief Ganger Ben Trounson had, of course, not the slightest notion of the part they had played in the tragedy and carried on their work obliviously, with a perfectly clear conscience.

18 - V is for vengeance (June 1944)

Immediately after the Normandy Landings in France, the people of Britain had really begun to feel that the end of the War was coming into sight and that Germany's time was running out. The Russians were slowly overwhelming the Wehrmacht armies in the East; North Africa had been cleared and the Allied armies, now assisted by the reconstituted French Army, were fighting their way across France and Italy.

But the Britons, to their cost, were still to experience a most unpleasant shock: they had heard about Hitler's boastings of new 'Vengeance' weapons, although his angry words had not been taken seriously. The Allied military in Britain had been aware for some time of Hitler's lunatic orders to his generals, demanding the movements of German units which no longer existed. The Flying Bombs, however, were a completely different matter; these were no figment of Hitler's tortured imagination. There had long been suspicions about bomb-carrying rockets; the Allied air forces had paid special attention to the experimental rocket bases and had heavily bombed Peenemünde on the Baltic coast, where they knew experimental flights had taken place. Bomber Command had already obliterated the visible launching pads in northern France and had assumed that, after Normandy, rockets would not be in a position to attack the UK.

They were wrong.

Driver Alan Hampton glanced at Fireman Jake Harrison, who was looking anxiously out of the cab side of their general purpose Grange Class 4-6-0. It was early August and they were due to arrive with their mixed freight at Paddington Goods at 4.27pm.

"What's up, Jake?" They were only half an hour off the end of their turn of duty and all that remained was to leave their engine at Old Oak Common shed, spend the night at the local enginemen's hostel, and return to duty next morning on whichever train Control had organised for them, with the locomotive that the Shedmaster at Old Oak had allocated for the train. They both lived in Swindon and, while Jake was still young and relatively inexperienced, he seemed competent enough in Alan's eyes.

They hadn't been east to the London area very often, as their usual shifts had taken them to Bristol, Cardiff, Weymouth or Plymouth. Although Jake had already had a week to 'learn the road' to Paddington, and while the route between Bristol and London was very busy, there were no unusual hazards that might explain the worried frown on the young man's face.

"It's them flyin' bombs, Mr Hampton."

"Oh, the V1s! Don't you worry about them, Jake. There's no pilot in them, so they can't be targeted at us." Trains had often been attacked by Luftwaffe fighters or bombers but the Messerschmidts, Junkers 88s and Focke-Wolf 190s were very rare over British skies by this time.

"But our planes can't catch 'em, they're too fast, I've 'eard."

"Yes, I believe that's true," replied Alan, "but there's not so many of them, especially now that our lads are in France and have cleared up the launching sites."

"So what do we do, if we sees one of 'em comin' over?" Jake was still urgently scanning the sky.

"Do? Why, we don't do anything. Their engines have a funny rumbling sound and as long as you can hear that, you're perfectly safe."

"How's that then?" Jake stared at his driver, "'Ow c'n we be safe if they're over'ead?"

"Simple: if they're flying, they're not dropping. I've actually seen a couple belting along quite low. It's when the engine stops you've got to watch yourself."

"'Ow d'yer mean?"

"When the engine stops, they just fall and explode; so you have to listen carefully and when the noise stops, they're coming down, so you get under cover as quickly as you can."

"What if there's no cover handy, like?"

"Just drop flat and start to pray. And talking of praying, my steam pressure's dropping, so get shovelling or we won't be on time in Paddington, I'll have some explaining to do, and you'll be shovelling very hard on our next trip!"

"Yes sir, Mr Hampton, sir." Jake picked up his shovel with a grin.

"Cheeky young devil!"

They managed to arrive at Paddington Goods only a few minutes down, and Jake climbed down to uncouple the engine, which they then took back to Old Oak Common shed.

By late August, even Jake had become accustomed to occasional reports of V1s landing in the area surrounding London, although they were becoming less frequent. The Observer Corps were sighting them and guiding RAF Tempest fighter aircraft onto them, and these were sometimes able either to shoot them down outright or tip their stubby wings to direct them away from London as they passed, although this latter was a risky business.

In early September, however, a huge explosion occurred in the London area, which the authorities attributed to the bursting of a large gas pipe. But when two more occurred within weeks, there was a growing public suspicion concerning them. Yet enemy action appeared unlikely, as there were apparently no hostile aircraft about when the explosions occurred. Sabotage was equally implausible because the sites of these explosions seemed to be random and of no military value. It was thought by some that they were caused by accidents involving heavy explosives on the move in preparation for the Allies' imminent arrival on German soil.

But railwaymen were generally concerned with the more immediate matter of keeping time, with so many heavy military freight trains clogging the system. Complaints were rife at Old Oak Common shed: "The buggers are expecting miracles of us!" grumbled one driver to his mates in the messroom. "Johnny Brent and I just got in on a

Hereford express and it took us over eight hours. We got held up both at Worcester and Honeybourne, and then they rerouted us from Oxford through bloody Thame and we were stopped once more at Acton."

"Yus," chimed in a fireman, "an' I bet it were 'urgent freights' with tanks an' howitzers and God knows wot on board. We've had a few o' them as well. That's why we was eighty-six minutes down on the Weymouth passenger: we got stopped at Yeovil an' at Newbury they kept us while two freights went through from Didcot to Southampton an' jus' left us standin' there daft like a bloke watchin' 'is girl go off with a rich Yank!"

But Alan Hampton and his fireman paid little attention to the complaints. Expecting miracles had been the norm almost since the war had begun five years earlier and most railwaymen were used to it, but from time to time it got too much and a little steam had to be let off, even though most knew that management 'buggers' were also doing their best under extremely trying conditions.

Normally, Alan and Jake were on local or semi-fast passenger shifts from Swindon but one day they were sent as ordinary passengers (or 'on the cushions' in railwaymen's parlance) north-west to Banbury, to take a light freight from the LNER to Southampton via Newbury and Winchester. On arriving at Banbury, they were displeased to note that their engine was an American 'Austerity' 2-8-0. Although these wartime engines had comfortable padded seats, even for the fireman, they were fairly basic and were unpopular among GWR men because they were not as powerful as they looked, and could be unreliable. The two men discovered that their freight consisted of a dozen tanks and five troop-carrier vehicles, headed for Southampton docks. They were familiar with the road, which had been recently converted to double track and consequently there was no need to bother with single-line token collecting and depositing; the method by which a single stretch of track could only have one train on it at a time. In short, the duty would be a relatively easy one. Yet this shift was to produce a bad fright, to remind them that the war was by no means over. As they were crossing a long viaduct, Alan glimpsed a distant aircraft flying very low along the valley. "Hey, look at that low-flying Hurricane, Jake," he commented. "I bet the pilot's having a bit of fun."

Jake looked and then gasped, "That's not a Hurricane, Mr Hampton, it's a German Focke Wulf and he's gunning for us!"

"Hell! And we're too far from that tunnel! The sod can't miss us, we're sitting ducks! Get your head down, quick!"

Alan grabbed the engine brake and immediately the train began to slow down. The rattle of gunfire could be heard as the aircraft overshot the train, passing just in front of the locomotive. Its pilot swept up in a wide turn, clearly intending to come back for another attack.

Alan stared at his fireman, "I'm sorry, Jake, I can't see him missing us again, and there's noth—"

As he spoke, there was another deafening growl as two Spitfires roared overhead and up towards the turning enemy fighter. Its pilot instantly flipped his fighter on its back and dived, twisting as he flew directly underneath the two RAF fighters, catching both of them by surprise. Before they could turn and engage him, he was well away.

"My god, Jake, I thought we were done for then," breathed Alan.

"You and me both, Mr H." Jake was still shaking as they entered the tunnel at the end of the viaduct. "I can't wait for this blasted war to end."

But Driver Hampton and Fireman Harrison were to make further close and personal acquaintance with Hitler's vengeance. They had brought a semi-fast from Swindon into Paddington and had left their Castle class 4-6-0 at Old Oak Common shed, for turning and servicing while they spent the night at the railwaymen's hostel. It was only a ten-minute walk from the steam shed but as they walked a massive explosion shook the area. It occurred in the street 300 yards away and, curiously, both men heard a very loud roar reaching down from the sky immediately after the street explosion.

"What in hell was that?" gasped Jake as the fronts of several terraced houses on either side of the road began to lurch forward and collapse into the street. The two enginemen were far enough away from the blast not to be hit by the falling bricks and glass shards that showered down in the immediate area of the crater in the road.

"Come on, Jake," said Alan, hauling his fireman onto his feet. "Quick, let's hurry and see if we can help anyone."

His words helped to quell Jake's anxiety and the fireman lumbered to his feet, shaken but determined to assist if he could. However, they were both horrified to see several unmoving bodies on the road; two were small children, one still in nappies. There was nothing they could do for the dead, so they helped some of the less badly injured to where they could hear the ambulances approaching, bells clanging urgently. Several policemen and soldiers were quickly on the scene and a few uninjured passers-by were also helping those who were too shocked and dazed to cope.

An hour later, both men were in the hostel. "One of the coppers told me it was a V2," said Alan to the listening railwaymen.

"What the hell's a V2?"

"Apparently it's some sort of rocket bomb the Germans have developed."

Both men were sipping at small glasses of calming brandy the hostel staff had conjured up from somewhere, to the envy of other enginemen.

"Yer lucky bugger!" commented one driver, eyeing the brandy that Jake was holding.

This was the last straw for Jake: "Sod you, mate!" he shouted, and hurled the rest of his brandy in the man's face. "You just spend an hour picking up dead kids off the street after one of those bloody bombs drops. See if you feel lucky afterwards!" He stormed off out of the room.

Nobody else said a word.

19 - A train to suffer in (July 1944)

The long-awaited Allied invasion of the north of France had begun and the British, American and Canadian troops had established a firm foothold on French soil. The beach landings had been particularly hard for the Americans. They had met stronger resistance from the German defences than the British and Canadians had, but in spite of the early opposition, Allied soldiers were now deep into Normandy. There was plenty of heavy fighting and the German armies were putting up a strong defence. Consequently, there were heavy casualties on both sides. The French port of Cherbourg had been freed, and the wounded were being ferried from there to ports in the south of England.

The long, khaki train with its great red crosses on the white roofs and sides was waiting at the dockside in Southampton. It demonstrated, amongst other things, the close co-operation between the major railway companies during the War. The coaches were Southern Railway ambulance coaches, modified from standard carriages at their Lancing works, and the locomotive was a Great Western Hall class 4-6-0. The train was due to take the wounded from France north, via Winchester, Newbury and Didcot to Banbury, where it would be handed over to an LNER locomotive for further travel to hospitals in the Leicester and Nottingham area.

The train itself comprised of eleven carriages: one with an emergency operating theatre and medical store; one with a boiler room for heating water and general store; one for staff accommodation; one for sitting patients; six as hospital wards, and a brake van. The cab crew knew that they would need to manage this particular duty with care in order to give the wounded troops as easy a journey as was possible under the circumstances. Driver Tommy

Sefton and his fireman Seth Hapgood of Didcot had been selected for the duty because they were experienced and had taken hospital trains before, with appreciation from the medical staff.

As Driver Sefton eased his train gently out of Southampton, his fireman commented, "Did you see those three poor buggers being taken into the third coach, Tom?"
"Yes Happy, they went into the coach next to the operating theatre. I reckon the doctors might have planned to operate before reaching a hospital. We'll have to take extra care." This view was confirmed as they were brought to a standstill in Eastleigh and a doctor came up to them.
"We're going to have to operate, Driver. Three of the men can't wait to get into a hospital. We're going to try and stabilise them, which won't take too long; about twenty minutes each, I hope. This might keep them alive until they can get full hospital attention."
"Yes, Doctor, we saw them and will do what we can to give as smooth a ride as possible." The doctor nodded his thanks and went back to the operating coach. Although the train had a clear run with no signal checks, Tommy Sefton kept the speed down to give the operating doctors a steady base as they moved onto Great Western metals at Shawford Junction and came to a halt at Winchester. A nurse hurried up to the cab with a request for them to pause for ten minutes while a critical stage of an operation was carried out. "If they make the slightest mistake, the man won't live," she explained.
"Nip out, Happy, and tell the Stationmaster why we can't proceed for a few minutes," said Tommy to his fireman.
"Right-o." Happy climbed down from the cab and headed off to the Stationmaster's office. He came back a few minutes later. "The Stationmaster says that's fine, he'll explain to Newbury why the special will be a bit late."
The critical part of the operation took another fifteen minutes, then a doctor came to the cab. "Thanks, Driver, our patient's over the worst now that we've stabilised him. You can move the train again."

"Glad to hear that, Doctor, we'll get on again." Tommy released the train brake and as Happy unwound the tender brake the train began to glide away towards Whitchurch. Arriving twenty minutes late, they stopped once more at the doctor's request for another urgent operation before continuing half an hour later. This time, a nurse came out and thanked them but explained that, while the surgeon had tried his best, the soldier had not survived.

"We're so sorry to hear that," answered Tommy. "That must be a blow to the surgeon who tried so hard."

"Yes," said the nurse, "he was very upset, and he knows there will probably be several more before we reach the Nottingham area. Some of the troops are very badly wounded and their chances are not good."

"They're all British or Allied, I take it?" asked Happy.

"Oh, no. We have quite a few Germans on the train as well. We even have a German doctor. We treat wounded soldiers without worrying about which side they were on."

"Well good luck with the rest anyway," said Tommy as he released the vacuum brake in preparation for getting under way once more.

Leaving Whitchurch, Tommy was surprised to see Happy staring fixedly out of the cab at the sky. "What's up, Happy?" he said.

"I can see an aircraft circling not far away," replied the fireman. "I did some aircraft recognition practice with my cousin when he was volunteering for the RAF, and that there aircraft looks to me like a Junkers 88!"

"What? But surely he wouldn't attack a hospital train!"

"You wouldn't think so, but he's circling like he means business." Happy kept his eyes on the progress of the enemy fighter. "Blimey! He's lining us up, Tom!"

"The bastard!" shouted Tommy, staring ahead along the line at a tunnel a mile or two ahead. "Let's see if we can get to that tunnel before he comes at us!" He increased the speed but both crewmen could see that there was no chance of gaining the safety of the tunnel before the Junkers could open fire on them. They were on wide open land and there was little they could do to avoid the aircraft's guns. Just as the fighter began to fire, Tommy applied the emergency brake and the sudden slowing of the train threw the pilot off his aim, the cannon shells peppering the track ahead of them.

"I know what I'm doing to the poor buggers in the train," groaned Tommy. "I'll try and speed up if he comes round again. Rather than that have the whole train machine gunned!"

Happy nodded. "Yeah, and we might even have time to reach that tunnel. The bugger needs time to circle round and come at us again."

But Driver Sefton and Fireman Hapgood were spared from inflicting further possible injuries to their train's passengers. As the Ju 88 behind them began to line itself up to attack, there was a sudden rattle of cannon fire and the pilot of the Ju 88 swerved off to the right, followed by an American Mustang. Happy stared, entranced, as the dogfight developed. The German was firing back at the American but the latter slid sideways out of the line of fire and the Ju 88 pushed its nose down to try and gain speed and escape. The Mustang pilot, however, was an experienced flyer and looped tightly under the German, firing another long burst up at the belly of the enemy plane. Straightaway, one of the Ju 88's engines began to pour out smoke, and the machine immediately tipped sideways to begin a downwards plunge. Two black figures could be seen ejecting from the plane and their parachutes opened as they floated down. This was clearly not enough for the Mustang pilot and he repeatedly dived on the two descending crewmen and shot their parachutes to ribbons, before flying away.

The GWR cabmen watched in horror as the two black dots plunged to the ground about half a mile away.

"That Yank pilot was an angry man!" said the shaken Happy slowly.

"He was that right enough," replied Tommy. "But I can't say I blame him. Mind you," he added, "if the authorities saw what he did, he could be charged with murder, but they might argue there were extenuating circumstances. Our blokes don't attack their hospital trains, and they don't normally attack ours, either. The crew of that Ju 88 got what they deserved." Driver Sefton eased the regulator open and they gently picked up speed once more.

The next stop was at Newbury, where they were directed to a racecourse station siding so that the medical staff on the train could have a chance to check on their patients while the train was at a standstill. The shaking of the train during the sudden application of the brakes to escape the Ju 88 had caused a number of casualties, among both staff and patients. Two nurses had been hurt, one with a broken leg and the other with scalding, as she had been holding a basin full of hot water. Fourteen soldiers also needed emergency attention, and the pause gave the staff a welcome chance to render assistance where it was required. A senior doctor had seen the cannon shells exploding in front of the train and had understood why Driver Sefton had used the emergency brakes. He made a point of coming to the cab and thanking the crew for their prompt action.

"I was in the desert in '41," he explained to them, "and I saw for myself what cannon shells can do to a troop train. It was something I never wanted to see again, and especially not to an ambulance train. We are extremely grateful to you for your quick thinking, which almost certainly saved dozens of lives."

"Yes, well, you have to thank that Yank pilot more than us, Doctor. If he hadn't have turned up, we'd have been shot up. We were trying to reach a tunnel, but we knew we couldn't make it; it was still too far away."

"Yes indeed, we were very fortunate there; I suppose he caught that German plane, did he?"

"Yes, he shot it down," replied Tommy. He gave no further detail; if the American authorities did not know what their pilot had done, Tommy wasn't going to inform them.

"I notice you didn't tell that doctor about the Yank

shooting the German crew's parachutes," commented Happy as they coasted downhill in the approach to Didcot some time later.

"No fear," snorted Tommy angrily, "the sods deserved what they got! We've seen a few German aircraft when we've had other hospital trains and they've always left us alone."

Happy nodded slowly, "I still feel sorry for that pilot," he continued thoughtfully, "I think he might be in shtuck."

"Why?" demanded Tommy. "If we were the only ones who saw what he did, he's safe."

"But they'll see the holes in the German parachutes, an' they'll know damn well what happened."

A fortnight later at an American Army Air Force base, a green uniformed major was interviewing the Mustang pilot.

"Why were the holes in these guys' parachutes? How do you explain that?"

"Not sure, sir, I guess that must have happened when I shot into the cockpit of the 88. Some of the shells must've gone through their chutes. Only thing I can think of, sir."

"Curious how the chutes were shot through but the German bodies had no shell holes. And Lootenant, I don't like smartass pilots. Dismissed!"

"Sir!"

"Hmhh!" muttered the major to his staff captain as the pilot left the room. "Insolent young pup thinks I was born yesterday!"

20 - Suffocation (Jan 1945)

It was becoming very clear to most people that the war was nearing its end; it was generally expected that the Allies would move deeply into Germany. The Russians, after their successes on the Eastern Front and, above all, the surrender of General Paulus and his 90,000 men at Stalingrad, in addition to the major Russian tank victory at the battle of Kursk, were closing in on Berlin, with desperate German forces regularly failing to hold them back. The Allies were already across the German frontier in the west and final victory was obviously only a matter of time. Military experts on both sides knew perfectly well that, while the Germans could still occasionally surprise them, a total German defeat was clear to everybody; except, apparently, to Hitler. Yet the Germans were still fighting hard.

In the previous June, the Allies had felt enormous relief at finally and successfully landing in France against tough opposition, but in London any possible feelings of slight relief amongst the civilian population had been brutally stifled by the onset of the Doodlebug attacks. These had caused shock to the morale of Londoners (although very senior military figures quietly discounted them, as they very rarely hit valuable targets). Now the Germans had once more surprised the Allies with their sudden attack in the Battle of the Bulge in northern France.

On the face of things, however; after almost six years of war, denial and rationing, it seemed there were grounds for optimism. It was generally believed that another year at the most would see the end of the war, and then one could get back to the kind of life that many could hardly remember; one during which you could buy what you could afford, without the need for coupons and other restrictions.

In the meantime, the war had to be won, and trains still had to move vast supplies of military freight about the country; war materials as well as troops to the ports. Regular timetabled passenger trains ran often with long interruptions and general goods services took the lowest priority; such trains frequently had to spend hours in sidings, much to the annoyance of their crews. Long-distance freights could easily find themselves taking eighteen or twenty hours on a run that in peacetime could be expected to last four or five hours.

The elderly 3F 0-6-0 tender engine, with its slow coal train from the Nottingham coalfields to the capital, had been due for a crew change at Wellingborough. Driver Ron Smethwick and Fireman Leonard Finch had already been on duty for fifteen hours – almost twice their normal shift – when they arrived in the late evening.

"Where's our replacement crew?" wondered Ron, looking around the snowy scene from the cab in the refuge siding next to the signal box, where the replacements usually took place.

"Can't see anyone this side either, Ron," muttered his mate. "Hang on – here's somebody coming out of the box now."

The visitor was a foreman. "Sorry lads," he called up. "You'll have to carry on to Kentish Town. We've got no spare crew."

"Two more hours to London? Bollocks to that!" shouted Ron angrily. "We've been on shift for fifteen hours already and got no more grub!"

"Don't bloody talk back to me, Driver, I've been on twenty-seven hours and I've got four more still. You'll have to manage, just like I will." With that, he stalked away, back into the signal box. The two men groaned; they knew there were plenty of unknowns which could still lengthen their shift, but they also knew there was no point in complaining.

Both men were depressed; it was snowing and bitterly cold. They had tightened the tarpaulin over the cab; there was little danger of an air attack at this stage of the war, it was to try and keep as much of the snow and freezing cold out as possible. In this, it was surprisingly successful, although that could not be said of the locomotive itself. This particular engine had been built in 1903 to a Johnson design and was classified as a 3F under the Midland (and later LMS) classification system, meaning that it was a freight engine of only moderate power. The 3F had been largely superseded by a rather larger and more powerful locomotive, the 4F, but the demands of war had meant that the railways were keeping old engines serviceable long after they might normally have been assigned for scrapping. Even the newest locomotives were suffering. This particular engine was certainly better suited to the scrap heap, for the 3F could only plod along at a very sedate pace, even when the line was clear and the load was not unduly heavy.

"Cripes, Len," muttered Ron Smethwick, "I can't see us getting to Kentish Town in a couple more hours in this old kettle."

"You an' me both, Ron," replied his fireman, peering out of the cab and trying to keep the snow out of his eyes; the track had a sharp curve to the right and Len, shovelling on that side of the cab, was searching for the next signal. Normally, Ron would see the signals because they were generally on the driver's left side but these two men had been a team for a long time and understood each other well. The engine clanked along slowly and methodically in the dark night; the sound by now having a soporific effect, but at least the work on the shovel helped to keep Len active. Ron, on the other hand, was fighting to keep his eyes open. The two crewmen were both ravenous and very weary after their extra-long shift, but they knew it was useless to complain about it. They would just get laughed at in their mess because most of their mates were equally familiar with long and arduous shifts, and had been for the last six years. Many simply shrugged their shoulders and got on with the job, thankful that they weren't in the forces, fighting for their own lives.

Len suddenly gasped in fright, turned to Ron and yelled, "Christ, Ron, pull up! We've just passed a home at danger!"

Ron shook himself, grabbed the regulator and slammed on the loco brake, while Len wound on the tender brake. Fortunately, the train was moving so slowly that it was able to stop fairly promptly; even so, they were well beyond the signal and they could make out the distant rear light of another train, not too far in front of them.

"My god, we could've hit that train!" Ron was shaken at the danger he had put them into. "I bet that bastard Fred has already recorded that in his train journal!" Neither man had any time for Guard Frederick Wilson, who was known throughout the division for being a stickler for the regulations. His dislike of cab crews had increased ever since one driver had been so incensed at a negative report that he had jerked his short freight into movement and thrown the guard in the brake van off his feet.

"Yeah, he will have too, the bugger!" grunted Len, "but it's damn hard to see the signals in this weather. I'll back you up, of course, Ron, you know that."

"I do know that, Len, and I'm very grateful." Ron nodded his thanks.

"What if," began Leonard slowly, "what if we said it was a different home signal to the one in Fred's train journal?"

"Why would we say that?" Ron was surprised at the suggestion.

"It could cause the Divisional Inspector to wonder about the record in the journal. Anyway, we weren't too far over the section and in the snow the bobby might not have noticed; we weren't there long."

"You know, we might get away with it," said Ron thoughtfully.

In the event, another situation rendered the whole issue irrelevant.

Roughly half an hour later, both men were fighting the urge to sleep; the beats of the engine were slow but regular, and the heat in the cab had become stifling, due to the carefully tightened tarpaulin. They had been on duty for well over twenty hours by now, and had had nothing to eat or drink for the last dozen of them. Their engine was slowing down gradually, although neither man noticed this (elderly freight locomotives were not fitted with speedometers) and when the train entered the tunnel at Ampthill, it came to a very gradual halt. The smoke in the tunnel was heavy and was filling the already effectively airless cab. Ron on his seat was slumped against the cab side window, and Leonard was asleep on the cab floor, leaning against the other side of the cab with his shovel still in his hand.

It was in fact the signalman who finally came to discover why the train had entered his section but not left it. He had known it would be a slow train but when it still had not appeared long after it should have, he rang the bobby in the previous section to check with a verbal confirmation that he had seen it pass to enter his section. Receiving this, he wondered why the fireman had not followed the regulations and come to explain the delay. He peered through his window but of course, in the dark and snow, nothing was visible to explain the missing train. Informing his colleague in the box, he left to walk along the track and into the tunnel to see why the train had stopped; he was sure there had been no crash, as he had heard nothing and no other train on the down line had passed recently. He found the stationary locomotive steaming quietly and climbed, coughing, into the cab.

"Crikey! The buggers have fallen asleep on the job!" he breathed to himself. This was an offence which normally led to instant dismissal from railway service.

He shook Ron to wake him but the driver simply leaned over and crumpled onto the cab floor, so he called the fireman, who also failed to respond. He too sank to the floor. The signalman then noticed that the locomotive and tender handbrakes had not been applied; this was always done when a locomotive was to stand for a while. With a dreadful suspicion forming in his mind, he checked the pulses of both men. Neither had one.

The subsequent inquiry found 'death by misadventure'. The question of blame was not mentioned. The heavy smoke in the tunnel, the lack of oxygen in the confined cab, plus the very long shift served by both men, were all seen to be parts of the cause of the fatalities.

Back in their home shed mess, the deaths evinced no surprise at all.

"It were on'y a question o' time," said one old driver. "It coulda bin any on us. We've all bin there at one time or another!" His listeners nodded grimly; they all knew very well what it was like to be hungry, on a long shift, and with an engine that was sometimes a year overdue for maintenance.

The old man shook his head. "They was good blokes and an' a damn good team. We'll 'ave ter 'ave a whip round. Ah feel reet sorry fer their families."

Again, there were nods all round; each man thinking what might have happened to their families in the same situation.

Deaths due to 'friendly fire' in the military were known (and often officially denied); but after six years of war, all railwaymen had become accustomed to the fact that although they may not have been in the fighting services, their role involved taking their lives into their own hands, on a daily basis.

Technical vocabulary

Banking engine: An engine at the rear of a train assisting by pushing from behind.

Bobby: railway signalmen. The name derives from Sir Robert Peel's police force.

Brake van: small van at the end of a goods train from which the guard could apply a brake to assist the driver when slowing the train. In a passenger train, the brake van would be a coach with a section for the guard.

Brighton Line: Railwaymen's term for the London, Brighton & South Coast Railway.

Caley: railway slang for the Caledonian Railway.

Distant: a signal warning drivers about the status of the section following the one they were entering. (see also 'home' and 'starter')

Driver: the man who controls the locomotive.

Down: the direction from London. (see also **'Up'**)

Fireman: the man who ensures that the locomotive has sufficient energy for the driver to do his job. Earlier commentaries refer to the fireman as a 'stoker'.

Guard: the official in charge of a train; he was normally at the rear of the train.

Home: a signal indicating whether the next section is clear. (see also **'distant'** and **'starter'**)

Horsebox: a van specially fitted out for transporting horses.

Lanky: slang name for the Lancashire and Yorkshire Railway

Light engine: an engine travelling without a train.

Link: a group of drivers in a shed who were allotted to similar duties. The 'top link' drivers were those with the highest priority trains.

Motion: the set of coupling and connecting rods linking the driving wheels and the cylinders.

Pilot engine: engine which would be coupled in front of a train engine and used to assist with a heavy train.

Salop: railway term for Shrewsbury, based on the original Latin.

Semi-fast: a train which does not stop at all stations.

Starter: a signal (usually at the end of a platform) to indicate whether a train may move off to the next signal. (see also **'home'** and **'distant'**)

Stoker: see 'fireman'.

Stopper: a train which calls at all stations on its run.

Turntable: a large, revolving table in an engine shed. It permits engines to be turned round.

Up: the direction to London.

Appendix

Major stations and depots referred to:

GWR

Stations	Running Sheds
Paddington	Old Oak Common, Ranleigh Rd. (servicing only)
Wolverhampton	Stafford Rd (Passr.)
	Oxley (Goods)
Birmingham Snow Hill	Tyseley
Shrewsbury	Coleham

LMS

Euston	Camden
Birmingham New Street	Saltley
Crewe	Crewe North (Passr.)
	Crewe South (Goods)
Shrewsbury	Coleham

LNER

King's Cross	King's Cross
Liverpool St	Stratford
Marylebone	Neasdon

SR

Waterloo	Nine Elms

Acknowledgements

I always consider myself to be exceedingly fortunate in my publisher, Katharine Smith of Heddon Publishing, for her careful editing and constant support. Budding writers could do a lot worse than contact her for advice.

I would also like to record my gratitude to Dr John Ritter, whose meticulous checking of the tales I find invaluable. His technical knowledge and style comments correct some of my glaring errors.

Finally, it was my wife Christa who instructed me to get my stories off the Mac and into print, and she hasn't even demanded her share of the royalties – yet.

Printed in Great Britain
by Amazon